"Tell me you'll stop digging!"

Brynn's captor jerked her up once more.

A noise behind them distracted her attacker. All Brynn heard was a skull-cracking thud before her captor released her and slid to the ground.

"Avery! Thank goodness!" She gasped out the words when she turned and saw him.

He was already on the move, motioning her away from her attacker.

"Get inside. There is a patrol car headed this way, but I'm not sure you're safe."

Brynn nodded, but she paused, staring at the black clad figure.

Avery tilted his head. "What is it?"

She pointed at the figure on the ground. "The voice. It was... I don't know. It sounds silly, but it was familiar."

Avery looked around before bending back closer to the figure. He carefully removed the hood.

Brynn couldn't hold in her gasp. The person who had just threatened her with a knife was familiar alright.

"It's her." She shook her head at Avery. "The woman at the adoption agency who threatened me."

Sommer Smith teaches high school English and loves animals. She loves reading romances and writing about fairy tales. She started writing her first novel when she was thirteen and has wanted to write romances since. Her three children provide her inspiration to write with their many antics. With two dogs and a horse to keep her active in between, Sommer stays busy traveling to ball games and colleges in two states.

Books by Sommer Smith

Love Inspired Suspense

Under Suspicion
Attempted Abduction
Ranch Under Siege
Wyoming Cold Case Secrets

Visit the Author Profile page at LoveInspired.com.

WYOMING COLD CASE SECRETS

SOMMER SMITH

LOVE INSPIRED SUSPENSE

INSPIRATIONAL ROMANCE

LOVE INSPIRED® SUSPENSE
INSPIRATIONAL ROMANCE

ISBN-13: 978-1-335-58839-5

Recycling programs
for this product may
not exist in your area.

Wyoming Cold Case Secrets

Love Inspired
22 Adelaide St. West, 41st Floor
Toronto, Ontario M5H 4E3, Canada
www.LoveInspired.com

Printed in U.S.A.

For the Lord knoweth the way of the righteous:
but the way of the ungodly shall perish.
—*Psalm* 1:6

This book is dedicated to my dad,
who has always inspired me with his thirst for knowledge.
I have always believed you could fix anything, Dad.
Thanks for giving me your curiosity
as well as your stubborn nature. I love you a million!

ONE

The building before her looked more like a haunted mansion in a scary movie than a respectable adoption agency.

Brynn Evans shivered involuntarily, checking the address in her phone once again. It read 2475 North Pecan Street. This was definitely it, but any good feelings she had harbored about coming here had long since fled. Had her adoptive parents really come *here* two and a half decades ago to find and adopt her? She wished they were here now so that she could ask them.

She reminded herself that the building had probably aged a great deal since then. Tall, rounded turrets jutted up into the sky, ending in spike-like spires at either end of the building. She half expected to see a pair of gargoyles standing guard between them. Russet brick crumbled around intimidating stone steps, and grass that had gone far beyond a need for trimming wedged its way up through crevices in the concrete surrounding a walk-out basement. Windows encrusted with dust lined the lower edges of the structure and Brynn could almost imagine eyes trying to peer out of them from the musty old basement. The windows on the rest of the structure weren't much cleaner, just a great deal larger and more forbidding. Very little light came through the ancient wood blinds, though dusk was falling on the quiet street around her.

She gathered her courage and made her way up the steps. She hadn't come all this way to be intimidated by a creepy old house. A heavy oak door adorned with an ancient iron knocker stood sentry at the entrance. She eased the door open and stepped inside, a rush of damp and chilly air raising goose bumps on her arms. Brynn paused, letting her eyes adjust to the dimness inside the house.

A voice called out from behind a desk, hidden in the gloom.

"May I help you?"

A pair of wire-rimmed glasses framed overly large blue eyes, cold and unfriendly in their assessment of Brynn.

"Um. I hope so. I'm looking for my birth parents and information I found reported this as the agency where I was, uh, adopted. I'm looking for an employee here named Suzanne Davis. My adoptive mother mentioned she was the social worker who handled my adoption when I was an infant, but that's all I could learn. I spoke to someone on the phone, but I was told they couldn't speak to me about it. I thought maybe if I could come in and prove who I was…" Brynn felt like her voice was overly loud and cheery in the tomb-like atmosphere.

The receptionist frowned up at her from her desk chair. "There's no one here that can help you. I suggest you give up your search and move on."

She turned back to typing on a screen before her, obviously expecting Brynn to just leave.

She wasn't giving up that easily, though. "Please. Is there anyone here who might know her? Do you possibly have old records that might help me? I'd really like to find my birth parents."

The cold eyes returned to assess Brynn for a long, uncomfortable moment before the receptionist spoke again. "There's something you should understand, miss. Some birth parents shouldn't be found."

Brynn fell back in surprise. There was such venom in the woman's tone. What was that about? What had she done wrong?

"I don't understand. You don't even know who I am." Brynn shook her head in consternation.

"I know who you are. It's best if you leave, miss, and don't come back. It's best for everyone." She pulled off her glasses and fixed her with a long stare.

Before Brynn could find the words to respond, the receptionist got up from her chair and made her way to the door. She opened it and stood glaring at Brynn until she walked blindly through it, gawking at the rude woman the whole time.

A heavy thud announced that the oak portal had closed firmly behind her. A gust of wind whipped her honey-blond hair around her face, and Brynn felt like something tangible was urging her away from this place.

Lord, why did You lead me here? She uttered the silent prayer but knew instinctively it wasn't something that would be answered right away. She would have to be patient on this one. She stumbled back down the run-down steps.

It wasn't as if she didn't have a next step to her plan. Once she learned she was adopted, Brynn had decided she might need to consult with someone to help her find her birth parents. She had learned that an old high school acquaintance worked in her former hometown as a private investigator. Her next move would be to get in touch with Avery Thorpe. Forget the fact that her heart pounded at the thought of seeing him again. He seemed the most likely person to help her. Besides, she had learned her lesson where matters of the heart were concerned. Her heart couldn't be trusted to fall for the right sort of man, it seemed. Even if Avery Thorpe had always been the kind of guy dreams were made of.

As she pulled up the address to Avery's offices on her phone, her thoughts returned to what had just happened at Cargill House. The woman had said she knew who she was. Was she the person Brynn had spoken to on the phone? Did she somehow recognize her otherwise?

Before she could ponder the thought further, a shadow fell across her path. She looked up but saw only a passerby meandering across the street.

She took a deep breath.

It was only a few more yards to her car, but she felt eyes on her, like someone was following her. Was the woman from the adoption agency coming after her to make sure she left? Had she come out through another entrance in the back of the house?

Brynn looked around her anxiously but kept walking, eyes moving and senses on the alert. Her thoughts spun about her like a whirlpool in a storm. What could she do now?

Pulling her phone out, she debated whom to call. The police would likely think she was just being overly suspicious. But she didn't really have anyone else to call for help. She was still twenty miles from the town of Corduroy where she had once lived. Even so, it had been so long since she had lived there that she couldn't really see herself calling anyone there now. She knew no one.

She had been barely sixteen when her adoptive parents, Stephanie and Blake Evans, had moved her to Greenville, Texas, for Blake to change jobs. He had died less than a few years later in a tragic car accident. Brynn had finished college and helped support herself and her mother with her teaching salary until Stephanie had passed away in March, leaving Brynn alone in the house they had all once lived in as a family. She had recently convinced her friend Tilley Watson, another teacher at West Bentley Street Junior High, to come be her roomie. They had connected as soon as Brynn started working there and had been close friends ever since.

And Tilley was the only person she had in the world right now. The only person who even knew where Brynn had gone.

Brynn slid behind the wheel of her little Mazda and locked the doors. If she could just get out of here, she could get to Corduroy. Avery would know what to do. She knew he would protect her, even if it had been years since she had seen him.

Maybe she should let him know she was coming. She searched up his number quickly and punched it in, thankful she had saved it when she looked it up earlier. The cell phone was ringing through her Bluetooth system as she pulled out of the parking place. She kept her eyes moving, watching for anything suspicious.

The call went to his voice mail. Her heart pounded like a schoolgirl's as she heard his voice asking her to leave him a message.

"Hi, Avery. This is Brynn Evans. I know it's been a long time, but I was hoping I might be able to enlist your help. I wondered if I could come by your office and speak to you. Today, if that's possible."

She left her phone number and disconnected. She had hoped for confirmation that he was there.

Brynn immediately began to fear his reaction. What if he read more into her request for help than a simple business arrangement? It wouldn't be the first time her naivete had gotten her into a scrape. She was often too trusting, and it landed her in a mess with men who had less than honorable intentions. Brynn had learned that too harshly recently with a man she had believed to be genuinely interested in a future with her.

He had turned out to be hiding a wedding ring.

Of course, unless he had changed a great deal since she last knew him, she couldn't imagine Avery Thorpe being anything but trustworthy.

Brynn followed the directions from her GPS because it had been a few years since she had been in this area. She had an aunt who still lived nearby, but Aunt Martha usually came to Texas to visit. Once her parents passed, the ties had weakened a little more as well. She made a mental note to visit Aunt Martha before leaving town.

A dark vehicle in her rearview mirror eased closer, and Brynn eyed it warily. Where did that car come from? Was she being followed?

The driver kept enough distance between them that Brynn couldn't make out any features. To be sure, she sped up a bit.

The car stayed with her.

Her pulse kicked up a notch. Unsure of what to do, she uttered a quick prayer. *Lord, get me safely to help.*

Brynn kept up a steady speed, watching the car and praying it would turn off somewhere. It didn't.

When her phone rang through the Bluetooth system, she answered it a bit too loudly.

Tilley spoke through the line. "Hey, Brynn. Did you make it to Wyoming?"

"Um, yes. I'm here. I'm on my way to Avery Thorpe's office." She could hear the tremor in her voice.

Tilley noticed right away. "Is everything okay?"

"I'm not sure. I think I'm being followed. The woman at the adoption agency was... odd." Brynn thought the car was coming closer, though still not near enough to see well.

"What do you mean?" Her friend sounded concerned.

"She practically kicked me out. Said some birth parents shouldn't be found, or some such remark. I don't know why she would have me followed, though."

Tilley was quiet for a moment. "Maybe she just wanted to make sure you left town?"

But she didn't sound convinced. Brynn wasn't, either. "Maybe. I'm glad you're on the line, though. It's still a ways to Avery's office. It will help to have someone to talk to."

"Isn't it convenient that the dreamy Avery Thorpe is a private investigator. Just the person to help you." Tilley teased. She had heard about Brynn's schoolgirl crush on Avery many times.

"Oh, come on, Till. He never looked my way. Why would he be interested now?"

"Things change, you know. And at least you're giving him the opportunity to get to know you. It might work out." Tilley's voice held the thrill of hope for a friend.

Brynn verbally waved it off with a sigh. "Not gonna happen."

Tilley let it go. She questioned Brynn about the details of her encounter at the adoption agency. Brynn thought she was just making conversation to help her stay calm rather than being seriously interested in some of the fine details.

It seemed ages before she pulled into the little Western town of Corduroy. When she did, she breathed a sigh of relief. "I'm here, Till. I am about to park in front of Avery's office and go inside. I'll call you when I leave."

Tilley agreed and Brynn disconnected. As she put her car in Park, she watched the dark sedan that had been behind her the whole way cruise on by. She hoped they were headed out of town.

Taking her purse, she closed the car door and stepped onto the sidewalk that ran the length of the street. An old building had been carefully restored to city code stood before her, and just as she had hoped, Avery's name graced the sign.

She couldn't help wondering how a private investigator could make a living out here. It was a pretty small town.

The street was quiet also, and her platform tennis shoes sounded loud against the pavement as she got out of her car. Another car hushed past on the way through downtown, but no one was out on the sidewalk.

She stood next to her car for a moment, shivering at the feeling of aloneness she had out here. Maybe it was just because of the events of the past hour or so.

Locking the doors, Brynn turned away to see the lights of her Mazda flicker in the window reflections when something else in the reflection caught her eye.

Someone lunged toward her. Her feet responded almost immediately. She was tearing away from him before she realized the door to the building in front of her had opened and someone had stepped out.

Brynn had barely realized she was no longer being chased when it registered that the man was now on the receiving end of pursuit. The hooded figure in a dark blue sweatshirt was fleeing down the sidewalk, running in the opposite direction, and chased by the man who'd come out of the building.

Brynn slowed and breathed a sigh of relief.

She reached for her phone, intending to dial 911. She didn't know who her rescuer was, but she was sure he would want some help.

She was about to press the call button and step into the building she had originally intended to enter when Brynn realized something that made her pause in astonishment.

The man dashing off after her would-be attacker was none other than Avery Thorpe.

This guy didn't know what he had just stepped into. Avery Thorpe was not about to stand by and let some bully terrorize a woman in his presence. As soon as he had seen the stark fear on her face through the window of his office, he had known something was going on. When the man had reached toward her, it had only proven his suspicions. It had already been a trying day, so the man was going to be in for a fight. The court case he had been working on had not gone as expected and he was going to have to change tactics on his investigation.

After bolting out of his office and startling the attacker away from the woman, Avery began chasing him in the opposite direction. Avery picked up his pace, sprinting hard as he rounded the corner where he had last seen the man. He slowed for a moment, then, scanning the area for the threat. The unknown figure ducked into an alley out of sight. He ran after him, but by the time he rounded the corner into the alley, the figure was disappearing out the other end.

Avery followed, gaining on the guy with every step. More than anything, he wished he had his Glock on his hip. He had been on the police force in Cheyenne for a few years, trying to make detective. He had worked his way up quickly but being a detective with the police force hadn't satisfied him. Working for the state as an investigator had been more fulfilling, but he wasn't there long before making enemies with the wrong woman.

That was when he'd decided to go into the private sector. Selena had taught him how to dig up the dirt on people. He just sincerely wished he had investigated her before falling for her.

But this guy… It was like a throwback to his days on the force. Avery ran after him almost gleefully, gaining ground and yelling at him to stop.

However, when the guy circled around and moved back to where they had started, Avery got a little aggravated. What kind of stunt was he trying to pull?

The woman was still standing near a silver Mazda coupe parked on the street. Why hadn't she gone inside yet, away from the threat? He suddenly understood the man's intentions.

The man was trying to go back and finish the job.

The woman was looking down at her phone from next to her car, and the man took advantage of her inattention. He raised a gun from his hip and fired. The glass of her car windshield shattered next to her head. The shot had narrowly missed her. She shrieked and dropped the phone, running for the cover of the building.

Avery was going to have to take a chance.

He dove toward the man, gaining speed just before jumping onto his back. He grasped the other man's gun hand first, trying to wrest it from the short, beefy fingers.

The man spun, trying to dislodge Avery from his back and still hold on to the weapon. But Avery had a fierce grip, and the man grew frustrated from his prolonged efforts. He squeezed the trigger and a shot fired, this time going up into the air. Avery clutched at the man's arm, but then he spun again, throwing him off-balance.

Finally, with a jerk, the man launched backward into the exterior wall of a nearby building. Avery tried to force his head forward, but the back of his scalp still made impact. His head spun and he lost his grip.

The man turned as Avery slid to the ground, raising the gun toward him. He grinned beneath the shadow of the hood shrouding his face.

Before he could squeeze the trigger, Avery swept an arm out and knocked one ankle out from under the man, sending him sprawling. He lost the gun and tried to crawl his way over to it. Before he could grasp it, Avery grabbed his ankle, preventing his advancement.

Just then, a patron emerged from an attorney's office on the sidewalk opposite Avery and the attacker. "Hey! What's going on here!"

The gunman looked over his shoulder, letting out an expletive. He snatched up the gun and bounded to his feet. As he turned away from Avery, his hood tumbled from his head, revealing dark hair, but he scooped it back up as he took off from the crime scene.

"Call the police!" Avery called out to the man, who plucked his phone from his pocket immediately. Avery launched himself after the attacker once more, but his slightly woozy state made it tougher to keep up with him this time. The perp jumped into a waiting black sedan near the corner and peeled away from the curb on two wheels.

The man from the office approached to check on Avery. "What's going on?"

"I'm not sure. He was shooting at the lady there." He explained what had happened, and when the police arrived, they both repeated their accounts.

Avery and the officer made their way back to the woman, who was now standing next to the door to his offices. He noticed that she'd picked up her cell phone. He saw her cringe at their approach and spoke soothingly to her. "Hey, we're here to help. Are you okay?"

A sniffle and a nod. "Is he gone?" Her wide-eyed expression searched his face.

"Yeah, the gunman got into a car parked around the corner and took off. I tried to see the tag number, but I was too far away." Avery helped her to a chair further inside. She straightened away from the door, reaching her full height, which wasn't much—maybe a couple of inches over five feet.

The officer asked her a few questions, and she answered hesitantly. She didn't seem to know any more than Avery did. When the officer left, she shook her head and sighed.

"It's not been my day." She brushed at the joggers she wore and adjusted her pale pink T-shirt.

"Oh? Has something else happened?" Avery looked around, wary of the vehicles moving up and down the street around them.

"Just a failed attempt to find my birth parents and some threats from a hateful woman at the adoption agency." Her focus shifted. "And now I'm being rescued by Avery Thorpe? I came to Corduroy looking for you." The woman was looking up at him with an inscrutable expression.

She knew him? He assessed her for only a moment before recognition flooded him. "Brynn Evans? You've sure changed."

She winced. "So I hear."

"I didn't mean it like that." His thoughts went back in time to the teasing she often took in school. She had always been a kind soul that hadn't deserved their tormenting. Kids could be mean, and her quiet, shy personality, ponytail and glasses had made her an undeserving target. She had endured it gracefully, but he knew it had to have hurt.

Unfortunately, he hadn't had the confidence then to stand up for her, though he had wanted to many times.

"It's okay. I know I'm not the same person I was in school." She smiled.

She didn't have to explain. Her composure and brilliant smile alone made him want to move closer to her. But neither was he the same as he was back in junior high. Though he had always been athletic, he also used to be too thin and wiry. He hoped she wasn't remembering him as that skinny teen.

"I guess you haven't received my voice mail yet?" Brynn's words turned his thoughts back to the present.

"Um, no, I've been a little busy with a case." He searched her face, wondering how much she knew about his present if she had found his website and phone number.

"I understand." She gave nothing away with her words.

Avery stared for a moment before coming to his senses. Here she was in danger and all he could do was sit here in awe of seeing her again.

She gave him a small smile and he almost forgot what he was doing again.

"I'm afraid I might be here longer than you'd like. My car…took some damage. I hate to go anywhere in that." She gestured toward the Mazda just outside the door and he nodded, looking at her shattered windshield. He winced, thinking about how close the bullet had come to hitting her.

"I can take care of that for you." He pulled out his cell phone, then paused. "If that's okay?"

She nodded and he put in a quick call to a friend as they walked back to his office. He explained the situation and the location of her vehicle before disconnecting.

"My buddy Will has an auto glass business. He's going to come out and get it repaired for you." He slid the phone into a pocket.

She looked surprised. "Tonight?"

Avery just nodded. "I figured you would

need it soon. He's a good guy. Always willing to help."

She nodded. "That's perfect. I'm glad you're still here. It's getting late. I was afraid I might not catch you before you left."

"I usually work late when I'm on a big case, and I have a court proceeding that isn't going as my client and I would like. I saw you through the window. Want to tell me what's going on?" Avery gestured to a plush side chair opposite a large cherry desk while he settled into a chair of his own.

Brynn took a deep breath before launching into the tale. "I'm a little confused myself, to tell you the truth. I just recently learned I was adopted. My parents—adoptive parents, I mean—didn't tell me for years. My father died in a car accident several years ago, and my mother recently died of cancer. Just before she passed, she decided I should know the truth. I tried to ask her why they hadn't told me, but she said they thought it was for the best. I didn't understand what that meant, but now I wonder. I was able to figure out the agency that handled my adoption, but when I tried to speak to the woman there, she told me to leave it alone. She practically ran me out."

Avery sucked in a breath, lips pressed together tight. Sympathy filled him, as he realized she had lost her family. "And then you were followed and almost attacked."

Brynn grimaced. "Yes. Something strange is going on. I'm not sure I can afford your services—I'm a junior high teacher—but I can make payments, if we can work something out. I've petitioned the court to release my adoption records, but they've declared that my need isn't sufficient to disclose the privacy of my birth parents. They didn't give me much information. I need your help."

He waved away her concern. "Payment isn't an issue. Keeping you safe if much more important."

Her fearful expression eased a bit. "I know I should probably do as she suggested and leave it alone. But I just…can't. It's too much of a shock."

"I don't blame you. I wouldn't be able to let it go, either. Let's get down some facts and we'll see what we can do, okay?" Avery suddenly wanted to figure this out for her more than anything. For one, this seemed like a simple case. There shouldn't be much involved in finding the identity of her birth parents. But also, he wanted to help her. His thoughts turned to the sweet, quiet girl she had been when they were in school. Her kindness had drawn him then, and it drew him still. He didn't like seeing that confused, hunted expression on her lovely face.

He took down notes as she told him about the Cargill adoption agency and what her adoptive mother had told her just before she died. But his thoughts kept straying to how expressive she was, how the light from the window shone on her golden hair, and how much he wanted to protect her.

He was going to have to get a hold of himself real quick.

After they had finished with a few of his most pressing questions, Avery stood. "I don't know about you but I'm getting hungry. Can we continue our conversation over some food?"

"That sounds great." Brynn smiled.

"There's a terrific little place right next door to my offices if you're up for a meal." Avery gestured in the general direction.

He directed her to the quiet café on the corner beside his building. The street beyond the windows looked like it had fallen right out of an old Western. The place was empty save for a lone waitress hovering near the counter. He waited for Brynn to slide into the booth before taking a seat opposite her. He couldn't say he was sorry to see her. He had always liked Brynn, though they had been barely more than acquaintances in school.

He thought back to her shy teenage years. He had been fascinated with her but hadn't had the courage to strike up a friendship with her. She had been the smart girl who was kind to everyone, even those who didn't reciprocate. But he hadn't a clue how to approach her. After all, he came from a cattle family and her parents had raised her in town. He had always feared they wouldn't have much in common and he wouldn't know what to talk to her about. The truth was, he had been a little timid, too, back then, even though his older brothers had been popular and that had carried over to him somehow. He didn't think most people had ever known how uncomfortable he'd felt around people.

Avery had soon learned, though, that being shy and quiet could be an asset. His older brothers talked a lot, sometimes forgetting he was around, and he learned many things that way. They were often surprised by details he knew simply because he listened.

He eventually gained a little more confidence once he got out from under the shadow of his older brothers. College had proven him capable and when he went into law enforcement, he had advanced quickly, becoming aware of abilities he hadn't known he possessed—staying calm under pressure, being empathetic, and always being able to read people. But that self-assurance had taken a hit when he botched a case. It had made a mess of his personal life as well.

He wondered if maybe his whole work-life balance was skewed. Either way, he felt he had lost credibility because of it.

He pulled himself from his dark thoughts and they ordered drinks from the young waitress, who brought them right away. Brynn was twirling her straw and he thought she was probably fretting over the whole situation. Her expression was melancholy now. It was better than being afraid, but he still wanted to make it easier for her. "We'll get to the bottom of this. I'll make sure of it. Where're you staying tonight?"

She looked at her soda. "I just planned on getting a hotel room or something."

Avery shook his head. "I don't think you should be alone right now, all things considered. I recently bought a house, but it's being renovated. I'm staying at Camille Classen's B and B right now and she has a couple of open rooms. Why don't you come stay there?"

He would feel better if he could keep an eye on her as well, but he didn't say that. He also knew that Camille would mother Brynn like she did everyone else, and he suspected she could use some of that right about now.

Brynn seemed to be pondering the idea. "Is it terribly expensive? I know her place is nice and, honestly, I can't spend my whole savings on this adventure."

"She's very reasonable, but your safety is the main concern." He didn't really know what her budget was, but he silently decided he would talk privately with Camille and take care of part of Brynn's bill to make it more affordable for her. If he knew Camille, though, she would likely lower her usual rate as an exception in Brynn's case once she knew the story.

Brynn finally nodded. "Okay. I'll at least check into it."

"I don't know about you but I'm starving. The roast beef sandwich here is delicious." Avery closed the menu the waitress had slipped him a moment ago. He waved the waitress over when Brynn agreed it sounded great.

They ordered sandwiches and fries and Avery leaned in closer. "Is there anything else you know about your adoption so far?"

She made a face. "Not really. I don't even have names for my birth parents. I'd hoped to get them at the adoption agency. My adoptive mom mentioned Cargill House and Suzanne Davis to me before she passed, but she didn't give me any other details. I was too shocked to think clearly about what to ask her."

"It might take some digging. I'm not sure the woman at the adoption agency will talk, though, given her reaction to your arrival earlier. We might have to try a different route." Avery was curious to know who this receptionist was and what was going on. Brynn's case had him intrigued already.

Brynn had opened her mouth to respond when a shadow crossed the window. Avery didn't think much about it, but when he turned to look, the flash of a dark figure caught his eye. Something about the way it moved didn't sit well with him. Brynn froze in her seat, face going pale at Avery's words as he got up.

"Stay here," he ordered. "Someone's watching us."

TWO

Brynn really wanted to follow Avery, but she forced herself to wait, peering out the double-paned glass to try and see where he had gone. She wasn't only curious, but she was concerned about him. And she felt alone and vulnerable without him close.

She couldn't see much of anything now that dark had fallen, so when a shadow appeared near the window, she didn't know if it was him or her attacker. Brynn slowly slid from the booth and backed away from the window toward the counter She looked around the café and found it was empty. The waitress had disappeared into the kitchen and hadn't returned. Where were all the people in this town?

Where was Avery?

The creepy feeling of being watched remained, and the seconds ticked by with no sign of Avery. She was debating picking up the phone to call the police. She probably should have already. But she wasn't sure there had been anyone there.

Should she go check on Avery or stay here like he'd told her to? What if he needed help?

The door opened, and Brynn waited, expecting to see Avery reentering the café. When someone in a hood slipped in, head down, Brynn frantically started looking for somewhere to hide. Where had the waitress gone? And why was there no one else in the whole restaurant?

She stumbled toward what she hoped was the restroom, praying to find a door that locked, but before she could get her feet to move fast enough, the figure rushed at her. An arm snaked around her waist, pulling her toward the front door. She tried to struggle away, but she was overpowered and shoved outside the door and into the shadows.

"We need to talk." The words were little more than a sharp hiss close to her ear. Cold fear trickled through her.

She shook her head to refuse the command, but the glint of metal drew her attention as a sharp blade settled near her throat. "What do you want?"

She shivered as the hooded figure pulled her deeper into the shadows toward the alley. She wished the waitress or someone would appear and help her, but still, no one else stirred in the quiet café. Had this person somehow harmed the waitress also? Was someone else working with her hooded attacker? Fear clawed at her as she realized it was up to her alone to escape her assailant.

If only she could find Avery. What if it had been a trap and he was lying somewhere injured? She thought furiously, desperate to come up with a plan.

She tried to look around, but the blade bit into her neck. She winced and tried to stay as still as she could while walking backward at the insistence of her captor. Another hand around her chest was far too tight in its relentless constriction. It cut off her air, squeezing at her diaphragm until she couldn't get her lungs to function.

"No more looking for your parents, lady. You need to disappear. Do you understand?" The voice whispered into her ear. "It's not a game. If you want to live, let it go."

Brynn started to struggle, but then realized the futility of the idea. "Why? Who are you?"

The grip around her tightened and her captor shook her slightly, causing the blade to nick her just slightly. It was more frightening than painful, but Brynn tried not to scream. One side of the metal blade chilled her skin where it lay against her flesh and the gloved hand that held it squeezed where it wrapped her neck to position the weapon.

"It doesn't matter. It isn't me you have to worry about. If you don't stop digging into the past, you're bound to regret it. Leave it alone, or you might not live to care who your birth parents are." The words near her ear were almost as menacing as the knife at her throat.

The voice was low and Brynn stood immobile to keep the knife from piercing her skin. Her whole body was tensed, ready to run, but still frozen to the spot for fear of accidentally moving too much and slitting her own throat.

"I'm only trying to find out who I am." Brynn heard the quaver in her own voice. "Everyone has that right."

"It's not your rights you should be concerned with. You'd better worry for your life. I'm telling you, it is not a good idea to anger these people." The voice had risen in pitch. What was that about? It was almost like her attacker was frightened as well.

"What people? Who doesn't want me to find my birth parents?" Brynn wanted to know what could be so bad it could risk her life. She needed to know who to watch out for.

"It all needs to stay buried. You don't want to know them. They won't take kindly to you looking for your birth parents." Her captor jerked her up tight once more. "Tell me you'll stop digging!"

A noise behind them distracted the assailant before Brynn could answer. All Brynn heard was a skull-cracking thud before her captor released her and slid to the ground.

"Avery! Thank goodness!" She gasped out the words when she turned and saw him. She reached to hug him, but he was already on the move, motioning her away from her attacker.

"Get inside. There's a patrol car headed this way, but I'm not sure you're safe." Avery looked at the figure slumped on the ground. "There was another one, but I don't know where he went. No doubt he led me off to give this one a chance to get to you."

Brynn nodded, but she paused, staring down at the black-clad form. A hood covered the head, dark glasses had slipped to one side, and a black bandanna was pulled high on the person's nose.

Avery tilted his head. "What is it?"

She pointed at the figure on the ground. "The voice. It was… I don't know. It sounds silly, but it was familiar. Something about it."

Avery bent to examine the attacker, making sure to kick the knife away from the unconscious figure's grasp before getting too close.

"I think… I think it's a woman." Brynn's words weren't much louder than a whisper.

Avery looked at her in surprise. "A woman?"

He looked around before bending back closer to the figure. He carefully removed the hood and then tugged the bandanna from around the face. He sat back where Brynn could see. "You're right. It's a female."

Brynn couldn't hold in her gasp. She had been right. The person who had just threatened her with a knife was familiar all right.

"It's her. The woman from the adoption agency." She looked questioningly at Avery. "Why would she come after me again? She's already threatened me. What could be so important she had to warn me away again?"

Avery frowned. "I don't know. But when she wakes up, I fully intend to find out."

"I don't know who she was talking about, but she said something about others not being happy about me digging into the past. She said I didn't want to anger these people. Do you think my birth parents could be in danger?" Brynn looked off into the growing darkness.

"It sounds like it's possible. We're going to get some answers soon. I promise you that much." Avery followed her far-off stare. But the sirens approaching prevented further discussion.

The patrol car was pulling into a parking

space outside the café now, the red and blue flashing lights casting an eerie glow on the quiet sidewalk.

"Stay here, Brynn. I'll talk to the officers first." Avery gestured to the café. When he strode toward the patrol car, Brynn wrapped her arms around her frame.

The police would have more questions. Brynn swallowed back her anxiousness as she went back inside to wait. The young waitress was wide-eyed, standing at the door looking out when she opened it.

"What's going on?" she asked. "I've been on break." Her name tag said Josie.

"Just a little misunderstanding, I hope." Brynn turned. "I think they have everything under control."

Josie still looked shocked. "Nothing like that ever happens here."

Brynn tried to soothe her, telling her it wasn't anything serious. She asked the girl about herself to take her mind off the activity around the café.

Brynn was still talking to the girl when Avery walked back in.

He nodded at Josie. "I don't think we're going to get any answers tonight."

"Why not?" Brynn's brow furrowed.

"She's refusing to talk. She asked for a lawyer, and that was that." Avery did sigh this time. "There's nothing we can do about it tonight. I asked the officer to keep us updated. He's coming to speak to you, though."

Brynn couldn't hide her disappointment. All the strange things that were going on seemed to be connected with her birth parents. Why were there others who clearly didn't want her to find them?

Her frustration mounted. She knew the smart thing to do would be to let it go, but what if they weren't safe? Could she live with herself if they were in danger and she didn't try to help them?

The thoughts swirled around in her mind, and though she knew he was studying her, Avery didn't ask what she was thinking.

All she wanted right now was for all of this to make sense. If she could just get some answers, she could head back to Texas and go on with her life. She wouldn't be having these uncomfortable tender feelings for an old crush whom she had never had a chance with from the start.

The police questioned Brynn and Josie briefly before disappearing once more. It didn't ease Brynn's anxiety at all, though. Her appetite was gone.

Brynn and Avery decided to have their meals boxed up to take with them. The evening air was growing cooler as they made their way back toward where they had left their vehicles. Avery's friend Will was just finishing up with Brynn's window and she paid the charges before he left.

"Follow me to the B and B?" Avery gestured toward his truck, a black four-wheel drive that didn't have a speck of dirt on it anywhere.

She decided she didn't have a lot of other options. Avery was the only security she had to cling to at the moment. Brynn climbed into her car and prepared to follow, but her attention was drawn to her phone before she could put her Mazda in Drive.

A missed call from Tilley stared back at her. She called her back, and there was no answer, but there was a voice mail from her. "I'm worried about you, up there in a strange town all alone. Now you aren't answering my calls? Brynn, what's going on?"

The message ended there. Brynn disconnected.

She had no idea how to tell Tilley what was going on. She didn't know, either.

But she fully intended to find out.

Avery called ahead to talk to Camille as soon as he got in the truck. Just as he suspected, she insisted on helping Brynn out and promised to have her room ready by the time they arrived.

He pondered everything that had happened,

wondering if he was putting Camille in danger as well. There was no way of knowing how many people were working with the woman who had attacked Brynn, and the woman would probably soon be released, anyway. She would just need bail money, and something told him whoever had been helping her during the attack at the café would be able to provide that.

Nothing about it all was making sense to him just yet. The woman had threatened Brynn at the adoption agency, and had come after her again anyway. She hadn't even given Brynn time to get out of town. And why the continued warnings for Brynn to stop looking for her birth parents? Who were they and why would it put Brynn in danger to look for them?

As soon as he got her settled at the B and B he intended to start digging. Maybe his brother Grayson, a former US marshal, could help him out. Grayson might be able to find a connection from cases involving anyone with the same last name as Brynn or at least around the time of her birth and infancy. Brynn's digging around in her past might be a threat to someone for some reason. It was the only possibility that made sense.

Camille greeted them at the door to the B and B with a trademark smile when they arrived. She was a stately redhead with a gracious way about her that made her a perfect hostess for the lovely place. She had inherited the house from a great-aunt who had once kept it immaculate, but financial restrictions had almost made it impossible for Camille to retain it, until she renovated it into a bed-and-breakfast. Many clients, like Avery, stayed long-term for various reasons, one of which usually included her fantastic meals and all the little touches she spoiled guests with. It helped that the house had a Georgian charm about it, with its bricked-in large windows and columned porch.

Camille settled Brynn into a beautiful aqua blue room with gorgeous touches of pink, like the fresh bouquet of baby pink hydrangeas on the dresser. Avery had peeked inside on his way to his own room just down the hall. The clean lines and soothing hues in the spacious room would be just what Brynn needed.

In his room, he pulled out his laptop and took it down to the sitting room to work. He had a few questions for Brynn. He knew the names of her adoptive parents, Blake and Stephanie Evans, and now the name of the agency where she had been adopted. He would start there.

He was still digging through what he could on the internet, laptop propped up on the coffee table before him, when there was a knock at the doorframe of the French doors leading into the room.

"Come on in." He didn't look up at first, but when Brynn cleared her throat from the doorway, he sent her a smile.

"Camille said you'd likely be in here. I'm sorry to interrupt." She hovered there until he motioned her in.

"Not at all. I have some questions for you, anyway. I need to know your birth date."

She looked at his screen. "February 17, 1994."

He typed the year into the search bar. "Do you know where you were born?" The database he used for investigation was pricey, but it was very helpful in cases like this. It was used by legal firms and government agencies alike, and it had led Avery to what he needed to know too many times to count.

"I believe I was born in a Cheyenne hospital. I'm not sure which one."

He accessed the birth records from all the Cheyenne hospitals from that date and saved the names of parents of female infants born that day. There were twenty-five, which didn't especially narrow it down, but it was a start.

"I'm going to check local news records and see if there was anything significant that happened around that time. Do you know how old you were when you were adopted?"

"I'm not really sure. But I know my adoptive parents had photos of me with them from the time I was around three or four months old. When I asked about my hospital photos, my mother just said they had been lost when we moved to Texas. I didn't think much about it at the time." Brynn shrugged, still staring at the screen in deep thought.

She thought for a long moment. "I can check with my aunt Martha. She might have something, but I'm pretty sure I don't have any from the hospital."

She left the room to make a call and Avery began searching through news articles from mid-1994. It was tedious, but he knew it was his best shot if Brynn's birth parents had been involved in something that someone might want to keep buried.

He could hear the low tones of Brynn's voice in the next room. She didn't seem to be having any luck talking to her aunt, but she was probably exchanging polite conversation with her now. He continued to click through articles until something fascinating caught his eye.

He clicked around a few more times. The dates lined up.

He looked up when Brynn reentered the room after speaking to her aunt. "Nothing that she knows of, but she's going to check. She promised she'd call me later. She acted a little odd about it, though, to be honest."

"That's weird." Avery pressed his lips together. "At least she'll be thinking about it. Maybe it'll help her remember something significant."

Brynn agreed. "Anything helps, right?"

"It might help more than you think." Avery enlarged the article without looking up. "You said you knew the name of the woman who handled your adoption?"

Brynn nodded. "Suzanne Davis."

Avery looked through the article one more time, then clicked back to another article from around the same time and read again. "Hmm. I might've found something."

Brynn cocked her head sideways at him, brows furrowed. "What is it?"

"Can you hand me the list of new parents from your birth date there?" Avery gestured to the open notebook next to Brynn.

She handed him the list he had written from his search through the database and he read through it before looking back at his screen.

He clicked another link connected to the first article about a fire and felt his stomach drop when a photo came up next to a newspaper clip about the same incident. "I don't think you're going to be able to find your birth parents, Brynn. I have some bad news."

She was looking at him in confusion now

and he didn't know how to tell her what he had found. He didn't want to believe it, but there it was, right in front of him. They had to be her parents, because the woman in the photo was the spitting image of Brynn. The names were listed on the hospital records they had found for her birth date. All the facts he'd gathered lined up.

Unfortunately, the most important fact he had just discovered was going to complicate everything.

"Brynn, I think your birth parents died in a fire right after you were born."

THREE

Brynn knew the blood had drained from her face because she felt light-headed and dizzy. Her stomach clenched, and she grabbed the back of a chair for balance. She looked at the pictures he had pulled up of the couple. He was right. The woman could have been her twin.

"They're dead? Both of them?" She hated the quaver in her voice but hated the news staring back at her even more. Their names were listed, Anderson and Rebecca Carrington. They had died of smoke inhalation before firefighters could rescue them.

"Why wouldn't the adoption agency just tell me that my birth parents were deceased? It doesn't make sense." She shook her head.

"I agree. There's more to it, I'm sure of it. It says the fire was started by accident, but there are no details on the investigation." Avery turned his attention from the screen of his laptop and picked up his phone and tapped on it for a minute.

"The article says it appeared that the father saved the baby—that would be you—before going back inside, presumably to get your mother. The front door was open, and firefighters found the baby under a tree in the front yard inside a baby carrier." Avery was reading on his screen until this last, when he looked up at her.

"My father saved me and then died trying to save my mother?" Brynn scanned the laptop screen, where he was now pulling up more articles about it.

"It would seem so." Avery's expression was full of sympathy and her heart did a little squeeze in her chest. His blue eyes seared right into her being with their soulful stare. Her thoughts dispersed, leaving nothing but awareness of the man before her in their wake.

Don't do that, she begged her heart. *Don't fall for Avery. You always fall for the wrong guys. Twice fooled is too many times.*

She had had a crush on Avery for years back in school, but she had never been the kind of girl someone like Avery Thorpe would notice, so she had kept it to herself, always admiring him from afar. And recent attempts at dating had done nothing but prove to her she wasn't cut out for modern-day relationships. She was simply too old-fashioned for that.

But if Avery had been handsome before, he was even more attractive now. She had been trying so hard not to notice. His thoughtfulness and consideration made him that much more endearing.

"Is there any mention of how the fire started?" She knew he had pretty much already answered the question when he said there were no details about the investigation, but she needed to get her mind off Avery's finer qualities.

He didn't seem to notice. He was watching her face too intently, and she didn't know what to make of it. It was unsettling. "No, but I'll see if I can access any records about the cause of the fire."

Brynn leaned back in shock. She was a little overwhelmed by all this. "If we could just talk to that woman from the agency... She must know something. Why else would she have attacked me?"

Avery nodded agreement. "I'll see if I can find the cause of the fire, but first I'll try the local police station and see if they will give me any other information on her."

"Okay." Brynn proceeded to scroll through the various articles about the fire while Avery left the room to talk to someone at the police station.

It seemed the story of a child being rescued had been a big human-interest piece, because it had been picked up by some of the larger papers outside of Cheyenne, including some national newspapers. She wondered about her birth family then. Had her birth parents not had any family, or had none of them wanted to take on the raising of a child?

She did find the name of the fire marshal who had been in charge at the time, however, and made a note of it. If Luke Miller was still around, maybe he could remember some details about the incident.

Avery returned at that moment. "I couldn't get anything just yet. But I have a friend who might be able to help me out. Wilder Hawthorne is a detective at the Cheyenne PD and has access to records we don't have. He and I were partners and practically brothers on the police force at one time. Maybe he can get to the files from the house fire. I'll get in touch with him first thing in the morning."

Brynn felt her hopes flail a bit before remembering what she had just found. "Okay. I also found a name that might help us. The fire marshal at the time was Luke Miller. Do you think we could find him? See if there were any questions raised in the investigation?"

Avery's expression didn't give her a lot of hope. "I don't know. For some reason I remember that name, but it isn't a good feeling I get about it."

He began to search through his phone again. He looked up with a frown. "I'm not sure if this is the right guy, but I found an address. There's only one way to find out."

Brynn felt her stomach flip in anticipation. "We're going to talk to him?"

"I'll call first to see if we can catch him at home. If not, maybe we can at least leave him a message." Avery tapped in the number he had found with the address.

He held it to his ear for a couple of minutes before giving up. "No answer. No voice mail."

"What now, then?" Brynn still felt the nerves. She had a feeling they were on to something.

Avery stood for a moment in indecision. "I guess it doesn't hurt to go back to the adoption agency and try again. Was there anyone else there when you went? Maybe in the back?"

Brynn shook her head. "I didn't see anyone else at all. I don't think anyone else was there. The Cargill House address is the only one I found for Suzanne Davis, though. I assumed she must have a living area in the upstairs of the house."

They returned to Cargill House but there were no lights on. The tiny sign declaring the name of the agency looked as if it hadn't been updated since long before Brynn's birth. "If she's here, she's not stirring. Maybe she came in and went straight to bed. I'm going to try to get her to the door anyway. It's not quite ten o'clock."

She had risen well before dawn to make the thirteen-hour drive from her northern Texas town to Corduroy, so she could reach the agency before they might close. It felt much later to her.

He knocked first, but there was no answering movement in the creepy old house. He rang the doorbell a couple of times.

"I don't think she's here." Brynn finally admitted the obvious.

Avery didn't turn away, though. Instead, he stood there, seemingly deep in thought. "You might be right. Or she might just be hiding out. But we are going to figure this out. When I talk to Wilder tomorrow, I'll see if he can get a warrant. She might be more willing to talk if we find something incriminating. We're going to figure this out for you, one way or another."

Brynn was following him down the steps of the crumbling house, trying not to focus on his wide-shouldered form in front of her. He looked like someone she could lean on, for sure. Those shoulders seemed capable of carrying a heavy load.

He turned. "I'll look into Luke Miller a little more, also. We'll talk to him if we can find him. Keep in mind that the fire was a long time ago. He might not remember much."

Brynn nodded. "It's okay. We can at least try."

Avery had stopped again and was standing in the yard looking at the house. He seemed lost in thought for a moment. Finally, he looked at Brynn and spoke. "Let's walk around back and take a good look at things, maybe see if there are any lights on anywhere."

Brynn glanced around. "This place is creepy."

He nodded agreement. "Stick close."

They made their way around the darkened yard toward a shed in the backyard. The windows in the back of the old house were dark as well. If anything, the rear of the house looked even more decrepit than the front. The shed appeared to be in good condition, though, newer than the house and detached sheet metal portico. A heavy padlock secured the door of the shed. That wasn't really all that unusual, though, considering it probably housed lawn equipment the owner hoped to protect from theft. It was still a bit sketchy, however, and Brynn cringed as Avery looked it over before peering into a dusty window.

"I can't see anything out of the ordinary." He pushed a hand through thick, dark hair.

Brynn didn't comment as they turned away, the darkness making it hard to make out many details around any of the buildings. She did wonder to herself what Avery hoped to find.

They walked back around the building, but still there was nothing unusual. She finally spoke up. "Is there anything in particular you are looking for that might help us?"

Avery slowed, glancing at her over his shoulder. "Just anything suspicious. I was curious about the shed in case it held any records, but I can't tell anything in this darkness, even with my flashlight."

Brynn pondered his response. "We might as well go."

She turned to head to the waiting truck.

Avery didn't respond. Brynn turned just in time to see him slump to the ground.

Brynn gasped, a scream escaping when a shadow stepped from the darkness. The sound of a cocking pistol echoed through the night just before a voice permeated the quiet.

"You should have left town while you had the chance."

Avery rolled to his back, the headache bringing the memory of what had happened back with a harsh pang. It was dark, but also too quiet. He knew on instinct that Brynn was gone. Why else had someone hit him over the head?

He lay there trying to regain a bit of coherence, but only for a millisecond before it registered that Brynn needed him. Now.

He jumped up to run for his truck, not sure which way to go. He changed direction for a moment and crouched at the end of the driveway to look for any clues. Shining the flashlight of his phone along the ground, he spotted some footprints leading away from the gravel drive. He followed them the best he could, until they ended near some tire tracks a couple dozen yards from the house. He ran back to his truck to pursue them. He commanded his Bluetooth system to call the police while he was putting the vehicle in Drive.

Once he had reported it to the dispatcher, she promised to send someone to help him track Brynn down. He slammed his hand against the steering wheel when he disconnected. This was his fault. He should have expected something like this. He had been out of police work for too long.

At the least, he should have waited until morning to undergo this adventure.

He was suspicious of the circumstances surrounding her birth parents' deaths right away.

House fires were not all that common anymore. Sure, they happened, but what really made him question everything were the other unusual incidents that had occurred since Brynn had started digging into her adoption. Something about it just didn't make sense. But what was really going on? Had the fire really been an accident? Were Brynn's birth parents criminals? He thought not. He *hoped* not. But something about the fire seemed highly suspect to him. The details in the article were vague at best, and he couldn't find any details about the couple other than a mention of their involvement in charity and Anderson Carrington's crushed hopes of running for mayor of Cheyenne.

Only two scenarios made sense to him. One, they had made an enemy of someone powerful that wanted them out of the way, or two, they had stumbled onto a truth that someone wanted very badly to keep hidden, badly enough to kill them to ensure their silence.

Now, as Avery sped down the street looking for signs of her kidnapper in the quiet town, he wondered about the fire marshal Brynn had mentioned. If the man knew anything, why would he have left it alone all these years? Avery knew it was possible he was just being suspicious, but it looked a whole lot like murder to him. The article had said the fire was an accident. But why wasn't the cause stated? And how thorough had the investigation been?

He wouldn't know until he spoke to Luke Miller. And maybe not even then. It had been about twenty-seven years ago.

Taillights ahead finally caught his eye and he accelerated in time to see them turn onto a road that led out of town. He punched the gas, hoping they wouldn't turn again before he could catch up.

It was the dark sedan he had seen earlier. It had to be the same guy who had attacked Brynn outside his office. Not the woman? From what the officer he'd spoken to earlier said, Avery had assumed she had been released. Apparently, her lawyer had arrived quickly and posted bail. And her accomplice seemed to have taken up her cause. Or were both of them working together again now?

The thought sobered him. If that was the case, he might need backup. He didn't want either of them to get away.

He put in another call to the local dispatcher to update his location and status. He also wanted to check on the whereabouts of the officer who had been sent.

The woman on the other end assured him the officer was close and promised to pass his information along.

He sped in pursuit of the sedan, hoping he could catch up before the driver became aware of his presence. He killed his headlights and punched it.

The driver slowed ahead, but there was no turnoff visible. What was the guy doing?

The sedan eased off to the side of the road, and Avery thought he might be stopping, but it suddenly zoomed off again. Had he finally seen Avery following him?

He accelerated until he was on the guy's bumper. It was risky, but he got right on his tail. The car brake-checked him, then sped off.

So he wanted to play games, did he?

Avery pulled up on the guy's bumper again, tapping the sedan with his truck grill.

The nose of a pistol poked from the driver's-side window in response.

Fear shot through him.

He could be risking Brynn's life. If he pushed this man too far, would he just shoot her and be done with it?

Please, Lord, keep her safe. Show me what to do. Avery didn't know what else to do but pray.

A warning shot bounced off his front bumper as he eased away from the other vehicle. The driver of the sedan took advantage of it and zipped away into the dark, shutting off his lights and disappearing into the hills.

FOUR

The sedan lurched, braked, lurched and kept accelerating, throwing Brynn around the back seat of the car.

What was happening? In her mind, Brynn was still replaying the terror of what had happened back at Cargill House. She had been standing at the mailbox when Avery had suddenly slumped to the ground, just before a thick hand wrapped around her mouth and the other, beefy arm had closed around her waist and dragged her away.

Brynn had kicked and struggled with all her might, but her captor was nearly three times her size, and he had wasted no time gagging her, binding her wrists and ankles, and tossing her into the back seat of an older-model sedan with fading paint. It had been too dark to notice what kind, but she didn't actually care. She just wanted to know how to escape.

And how long had it taken Avery to wake

and find her gone? Did he even know where to look for her? Panic filled her at the thought. She didn't know exactly what the man had planned for her, but it couldn't be good.

She struggled against her bindings, wanting to scream into her gag, though she knew it was futile. She also told herself not to waste her energy on fear. She would need to come up with a way to escape this man on her own.

The figure driving the car was dressed in dark clothes, jeans, long sleeves and a mask pulled high on his face beneath a dark ball cap. Shadows in the night finished the job of hiding his identity, assuring her she wouldn't recognize the man later if she had to.

Fear swelled through her. There was no doubt the man would use the gun, but where was he taking her and why? If they just wanted her dead, why abduct her? What did her captor intend to do to her? The possibilities made her skin crawl. She uttered a silent prayer for protection.

She could feel the car turn abruptly and speed away again just after the shot. After a few minutes of continuing at a breakneck pace, the driver finally slowed a little and eased into a cruising speed.

An expletive escaped the man as sirens sounded in the distance. He pounded the steering wheel and kept driving, accelerating once more. Would he try to outrun the police? What if he wrecked the car and killed them in the process? So many thoughts battled through Brynn's mind. Her imagination was going wild.

The pealing of the sirens grew louder and the car turned. Another string of expletives and the car squealed to a stop. She heard the driver's door open and felt a shifting of weight as he jumped out of the car. An officer yelled at the man to stop and put his hands up, but she could only guess he didn't obey. A couple of shots fired into the dark night. The empty driver's seat let in a blast of cool air from the open door and she shivered, hoping the officers would come find her quickly.

The back passenger-side door of the sedan suddenly opened, and she cringed, hoping it was an officer and not her captor coming back to drag her away with him. She couldn't see who it was from her trussed-up angle against the seat.

"Brynn?" Avery's deep voice brought a surge of relief. His strong hands reached for her bonds, and she relaxed as he cut through them with a pocketknife he pulled from his jeans. When he released the gag in her mouth, she gasped in a mouthful of fresh air.

"Avery! I've never been more relieved to see

anyone in my life. Did you catch him?" Brynn was scrambling to get her feet beneath her, for he had cut the ties from her ankles as well.

"No, I'm afraid he bailed and disappeared into the woods before any of us could get to him." Avery gestured toward the heavy stand of trees running alongside the road. "An officer is still in pursuit, but I'm not sure he'll catch him. Are you okay? Did he hurt you?"

Brynn was shaking her head. "No, just bumps and bruises."

Avery grunted. "I'm so sorry I let him take you."

Brynn winced. "Neither of us saw it coming."

He gave her a small smile. "I'm glad you're okay. We need to be more cautious, though. They aren't going to give up easily."

She shivered. "I agree."

He laid a gentle hand on her arm, and she almost forgot what they were discussing. "I'm going to be here for you no matter what."

A pang of longing hit her in her middle. She knew he hadn't meant it that way, but her heart didn't seem to understand. Those old feelings came rushing back. This was Avery Thorpe, the boy she had once thought all guys should be compared to. Even now, none had ever measured up to him.

Her expression must have betrayed her thoughts

somehow, for Avery cocked his head sideways at her.

"What's wrong?" He offered her an engaging grin.

She hesitated. "It's nothing."

"I'm sorry. I didn't mean to cross any lines." He studied her for a moment. "I will admit, sometimes I wish the situation was different between us."

Brynn felt heat flood her face. What did he mean? Her traitorous heart hoped he was feeling the same tender feelings for her that she was battling for him, but logic told her he could mean any number of other things. Surely he would never return her feelings for him?

She finally decided to just ask. "You didn't cross any lines. But…what do you mean about wishing the situation was different?"

He sighed. "I probably shouldn't admit this, but I've always liked you, Brynn. Like, really *liked* you. Being around you just makes me like you more. But I have to be honest with you. I don't want to get involved with anyone. I don't know if I'll ever want a relationship again."

Her heart squeezed with a tender ache at his words, but she squelched the thrill that shot through her. The feelings swirling inside her were just as contradictory as his confession. She was elated to find he had feelings for her, too.

And though she knew she wasn't ready for a relationship, either, she was hurt that he didn't want one. It was a paradox.

Brynn finally swallowed the huge lump in her throat and spoke. "I know what you mean. I don't want a relationship, either. I...well, I don't think I could trust anyone enough."

"I have the same problem." Avery sighed. "I was involved with a woman in an investigation several months ago. She was supposedly my informant for a very dangerous case. I developed feelings for her. That was a terrible idea."

When he fell silent, Brynn needed to know more. "She betrayed you?"

Avery looked at her and his eyes were full of pain and remorse. "She was playing both sides. I turned out to be the side with the least to offer her. I almost didn't get out of that relationship with my life."

Brynn made a face. "I'm sorry. That's worse than what I endured, for sure."

Against her will, her thoughts returned to her relationship with Aaron. She had fallen hard for him in a short time. Of course, he had done all the right things to charm her and make her think he was in love with her, too.

"I'm sure it was just as hurtful." Avery's blue eyes loomed close to hers, full of seriousness and concern. She found herself opening up before she meant to.

"I met what I thought was the perfect guy one weekend a couple of years after graduating from college. I had gone hiking with a friend of mine, and I turned my ankle. He was there hiking with his dog—a rescue German shepherd—and he helped me back to the car. He asked if he could check on me the next day, so I gave him my number." She paused, watching Avery's face. It didn't betray anything but empathy.

"We talked off and on for a few weeks. Then one day, he asked me out for coffee. Then for a lunch date. After a few weeks, I was seeing him almost every day. I never dreamed he was hiding something big." Brynn heard the catch in her voice and hated it. Why did Aaron's betrayal still have the power to hurt her?

Avery squeezed her hand and she remembered he was waiting for her to continue.

She had to swallow hard to get the rest out. "Then one day he'd forgotten his phone when he went to the bathroom and a call came through. I didn't mean to look, really. But the name Emily had popped up on the screen with a heart. The photo that appeared on the screen was Aaron standing next to a woman in a wedding dress."

Avery sucked in a breath. "That's a pretty big betrayal."

She just nodded. "He came back from the bathroom to find me staring at the screen and the charade was over. There'd been no need to argue the facts. The truth was right there, staring me in the face."

"Brynn, I'm so sorry." He started to pull her to him, but seemed to decide against it, releasing her. She understood why.

A uniformed police officer approached them then, nodding at Avery before turning to Brynn. "Could I ask you a few questions, please?"

Brynn suddenly felt very uncomfortable and honestly a little bit nervous. The police questioning just added to her anxiousness.

She must have hesitated a little too long because Avery spoke, low in her ear. "I'll be right here with you. He just needs some details for the report." He put a hand on her forearm once more.

"Okay." Brynn looked into his face, finding reassurance in his turquoise blue eyes. But his warm fingers on her arm distracted her, pulling her thoughts instead to the comfort she found there.

As the officer introduced himself, she worked to refocus her thoughts on the task at hand, steeling herself for the onslaught of questions from the officer. But her traitorous gaze kept straying to Avery Thorpe.

* * *

Avery watched Brynn carefully as she answered the questions from the officer. She had certainly put a knot in his carefully laid plans. Truthfully, he had considered giving up investigating altogether after a few recent cases, which had strengthened his suspicion that the local law enforcement was corrupt. He had run into more than one sign that led him to believe some of the cold cases he had been asked to take up were some sort of cover-up. He hadn't made any distinct or significant connections between the cases yet, but he wasn't sure he completely trusted the local authorities. He had made mention of it to Wilder and his friend agreed. He thought there were indications of corruption as well. They hadn't been able to prove it, however.

And maybe Brynn's case could be the one that gave them a link to whatever was going on in the local law enforcement sector. Before now, he hadn't had enough evidence to make a case.

But the danger Brynn was in trumped any concerns he might presently have over the lack of closure he was feeling about past cases and possible corruption. The attacks on her had made him lose hope about figuring out what had happened to her birth parents. If the department was incompetent, or worse, corrupt, they might never learn the truth. Or at least if they did, it wouldn't be without putting themselves in harm's way.

Brynn looked pale and nervous, eyes occasionally darting toward the trees as if still watching for her abductor. Avery wanted to offer her comfort, to shield her and make her feel protected, but he couldn't do that. She was in plain sight of plenty of people, with the other two officers at the scene. Their presence kept her reasonably safe, for now. It was only a momentary reprieve, however. Whoever was behind this, whether it was Suzanne Davis or someone above her in a chain of command, was determined to see it through.

Brynn looked visibly shaken by the time the questions from the officer ceased. She stumbled aside, standing wearily a few paces away and focusing her attention on her feet while the officer came over to speak with him.

"How do you know the victim?" The officer didn't mince any words. Avery glanced at his badge. Adams. He tried to place the face.

"She's an old acquaintance from my youth." Avery didn't try to hide his study of the man. Something finally clicked. "You seem very familiar. Do you have an older brother, by chance, Officer Adams?"

The officer pressed his lips closed and then opened them again to ask his own question. "So you don't know her well now? She tells me she just returned to the area earlier today."

Avery stiffened. He was torn between answering the question and asking his own once more. He finally chose to let the younger man's agenda play out. "I haven't seen her in a few years, no. But I will still vouch for her character, if that's what you're asking."

The man glanced over his shoulder, then sighed, his stance changing. He eased closer. "Look, there have been rumors for years. Everyone knows there are some things in this county you just don't go poking into. Strange that she reappears and someone starts shooting at her."

"Rumors? Then why have I never heard them before?" Avery leveled a piercing stare at him.

Adams stared back a moment. "Maybe you have. I'm just pointing out that this could be bigger than her birth parents. If no one told her she was adopted for all this time, maybe there's a good reason."

Avery narrowed his eyes at the man. "You don't think we've considered that? But she knows now. What would you do in her shoes?"

"Well, I wouldn't go sticking my nose into things that might get me killed." Officer Adams straightened and tried to look down at him. He couldn't pull it off. Avery was too tall.

"Wouldn't you? If it was the only way to get

answers?" Avery said it so calmly it seemed to give the man pause. Officer Adams's shoulders slid down a notch. He seemed to finally consider Brynn's perspective.

"She just wants to know who she is." Avery glanced at the woman under discussion still huddled a few yards away. His heart seized in empathy for her plight.

Officer Adams followed his gaze. "I guess I can understand that. But someone needs to keep her safe. Like I said, there are rumors…"

Avery nodded at him. "I'll see to it she's safe. What rumors do you mean?"

The officer paled. "Surely you've heard them."

Avery shook his head. "You're going to have to clarify what you mean."

Officer Adams shook his head and looked away. He looked uncomfortable as he turned to face Avery and opened his mouth, but before he could speak, another officer beckoned, and with a nod of farewell, Adams excused himself. The question he had previously asked forgotten, Avery was surprised when the man turned back at the last second.

"Rory Adams was my older brother, by the way. He was the same age as your older brother Grayson." He stuck out his hand. "My name is Brett."

Avery accepted his handshake, stunned. "I'm

sorry. I heard about his death a couple of years ago."

With a nod of thanks, Brett Adams was gone.

No wonder the guy hadn't wanted to talk about his brother. Rory was killed investigating a crime himself. Rory Adams had been a brilliant naval investigator who had crossed the wrong man while trying to find the truth. Avery's younger brother, Caldwell, had idolized Rory in his youth.

And the thought of Caldwell brought to mind another issue nagging at him. For the past several months, his relationship with his younger brother had been worsening. Avery felt Caldwell was on a path to self-destruction, but Caldwell didn't feel Avery was in any position to offer him advice.

It stung, but of late, Avery had developed a debilitating sense of self-doubt that made him fear his little brother might be right. He had seen too many failed cases and made too many bad choices recently to make him confident in his abilities.

Brynn shifted her weight, drawing Avery's attention away from his own troubles. He had, after all, just promised to protect her. Had she heard his hastily declared promise to keep her safe?

The familiar weight pressed into his middle,

making him aware of his own shortcomings. Could he guard her? What if he failed? What if something happened to her?

For a moment he considered asking Wilder to find someone else to take over. Maybe Wilder himself. Avery knew he could trust Wilder. She might be better off with someone else on the job.

But that thought made him feel even worse. He realized that what he had been brushing off as a lingering childhood crush was turning into something far more powerful. And while that might seem like ample reason to turn her over to someone else, he just couldn't bring himself to do it. He wanted to make sure she was safe, and he wanted to be the one to ensure that.

His feelings nagged at him. Maybe he was being selfish.

He had to get his mind moving in another direction.

"Let's get you back to Camille's and settled. You've had plenty of adventure for one day." Avery grinned. His pulse quickened unexpectedly when her expression brightened in response. He hadn't felt his emotions flare for a woman in such a long time that he had to suck in a deep breath.

"I agree I have probably taken this far enough

for one day." Brynn's expression betrayed her weariness.

"You do seem to have developed a knack for finding trouble. Is this something you've perfected over the years, or something you've only learned since your return to Wyoming?" Avery found he liked the way her lips curled up at his teasing. It only intensified the warm feelings for her swirling inside him.

"Oh, I think it started around the time you showed up." Her expression blossomed into a full-fledged smile.

He put a hand to his chest. "Wow. That hurt."

She laughed, and a very real pang hit him in the chest. But it was sweet and tender, not like what he had just mentioned.

He couldn't have that.

There was no room in his life for love right now. Maybe never. Attraction was one thing. But a woman like Brynn stirred something more substantial, far deeper and purer. It was something a man would have a very hard time getting away from. And sooner or later, Avery would have to get away. Because trusting a woman was something he could no longer do.

Their banter ceased on the way back to Camille's, and Avery wondered if her thoughts bore any similarity to his own. She didn't seem upset, but simply deep in thought. He decided she was probably just thinking about recent events and how they related to her adoption.

He had to admit, it was an intriguing puzzle. He supposed there might be any number of reasons her parents might have wanted to keep the information from her. But someone wanting to go to such lengths to keep the identities of her birth parents from her presented a whole new spin on the questions. And the rumors Brett Adams spoke of… Whatever they were, what could they have to do with Brynn's adoption?

He would do whatever it took to find out.

FIVE

Fatigue weighed heavily on Brynn's shoulders by the time they returned to their rooms at Camille's place. She longed to take a long soak in the claw-foot tub in her personal bathroom, but she opted for a quick shower instead, for fear of dozing off in the water.

But it wasn't to be. Before she could get into the shower, her phone began to sing out a merry tune. She groaned.

Aunt Martha's sweet face appeared on the screen, and she remembered that her adoptive father's sister had promised to call her back.

She answered the phone and Aunt Martha spoke to her pleasantly, almost as if nothing was going on. What was that about? Brynn's confusion was making it difficult to concentrate on the small talk Aunt Martha was suddenly making. Why was Aunt Martha acting so different than she had been earlier? Brynn was exhausted and couldn't make sense of any of it, so she played along with her aunt's niceties out of respect.

Finally, Brynn couldn't squelch her questions any longer. "Did you find anything else that might help me with my search, Aunt Martha?"

She didn't mention that they had discovered who her birth parents were. For all she knew, it might put her dear aunt in danger somehow.

Aunt Martha grew suspiciously quiet. Brynn waited as long as she could but finally prompted her. "Aunt Martha, do you know something you aren't telling me?"

A laugh came from the other end of the phone. "Of course not, sweetie. But I do have something to give you. Something from your parents."

"Okay. Could we come tomorrow morning? I'd love to see you." Brynn meant the words in all sincerity.

Her aunt hesitated once more but agreed at last. "Yes, I'll be waiting for you."

Brynn went downstairs to seek out Avery and tell him the news and found him still examining a page full of words on the screen of his laptop.

Brynn didn't waste any time with pleasantries. "My aunt says she has something for me from my adoptive parents. She said we could come first thing in the morning. If you don't mind going with me, that is."

Avery looked up at her with a charming smile, causing her heart to trip up for a moment. "I wouldn't dream of letting you go alone."

"Okay." She laughed, suddenly feeling silly. It had to be that mesmerizing smile. All the Thorpes had it. Avery just made use of it more often than his brothers. The other Thorpe brothers had always seemed so serious. The twins, Beau and Briggs, had gone into the military. Grayson Thorpe had become a US marshal, then later accepted a position as a security advisor for the White House. And Caldwell had always been something of a rebel, becoming a lawyer but then eschewing his law degree to work in the state sector as an investigator in Texas. But he still seemed more serious than Avery. Maybe it wasn't that Avery wasn't as serious, but he was more approachable to Brynn. The other brothers were a bit intimidating.

He pulled her attention back to the present. "We will leave right after breakfast."

They didn't talk much after that, and Brynn soon went to bed, exhausted and anxious to see her aunt in the morning.

Camille had prepared a delicious breakfast but Brynn's thoughts were on her aunt and finding out what she knew. When they finally left the B and B, she thanked her but she couldn't wait to get going.

Aunt Martha lived in a nice neighborhood filled with well-maintained older homes that boasted fine architecture and spacious lawns. She was waiting for them at the door when they pulled into the drive. She opened the screen door to welcome them as they ascended the porch.

Brynn accepted the tight hug Aunt Martha wrapped her in, her thin frame seeming less sturdy than the last time Brynn had seen her.

Brynn introduced Avery and her sweet aunt greeted him graciously, telling him she remembered his family well. She offered them refreshments and settled them in her cozy living room.

After talking for a short time, Aunt Martha sighed and began to look a little uncomfortable. "This is all going to sound a little strange. But your parents—that is, Blake and Stephanie— left a small envelope for you long ago. It was meant to be given to you if anything happened to them. And, well, now it has. I don't know what it is or why neither of them ever told you anything about it. I'd forgotten about it myself until you called." Her eyes were misty as she handed Brynn a small envelope that had been lying inconspicuously on a side table.

Uneasiness filled Brynn as she accepted the

offering. She held it, simply staring at it a moment before turning it over and opening it. When she pulled the slip of folded paper out, a metallic *clink* sounded. She looked down to see a strange-looking key on the floor.

Brynn bent to retrieve it, but Avery had already reached for it. He looked it over before handing it to her.

"A key? But to what?" Brynn looked at them both.

Avery shrugged as Aunt Martha shook her head in consternation, so Brynn unfolded the paper. "A letter?"

After a quick scan, she began to read aloud. *"Dearest Brynn. By now you probably know that you were adopted as an infant. There isn't much I can explain about the circumstances that led to your adoption. I can only say that it is all very mysterious. However, when we took you home, we found this strange key hidden beneath the fabric lining your baby carrier. Regrettably, we were unable to trace the origin of the key. But the fact that it was attached to your infant carrier made us feel that it might someday prove significant to you. We have asked Martha to keep it safe and pass it along to you should anything ever happen to us. Maybe you'll discover the reason it was left with you."*

Brynn wiped at the corners of her eyes and

finished reading the letter aloud. *"We have always loved you more than anything."* She missed them both so much, and the letter signed by her adoptive mother was a fresh reminder of her loss.

Avery looked away. He waited a moment before finally speaking. "I wonder if it could be for a safe deposit box. Many people keep their last will and testament in a safe deposit box. My father used to keep one at a bank in Corduroy and the key looked a great deal like that one."

Brynn studied the key again. "But how do we know what bank? What box? And don't you have to have your name on the register to open it?"

Avery frowned. "Yes, unless you are the executor of the will of the person it belongs to. Any ideas on who that might be?"

Brynn shook her head.

Aunt Martha pursed her lips tightly. "You know who your birth parents are?"

He looked over at Brynn, expression serious. It was time to tell her. Brynn gave a tiny nod. "We believe we do. Anderson and Rebecca Carrington were killed in a house fire around the same time we believe Brynn to have been adopted. The fire was reportedly an accident, but they never found the cause."

Aunt Martha sucked in a breath, but her expression wasn't as surprised as it might have been. Had she already guessed who Brynn's biological parents were? "Oh my."

When she said no more, Brynn speared her with a gaze. "Did you know them?"

Aunt Martha responded with a slow nod. "Everyone knew the Carringtons. They were good people. It was tragic when they died."

"No one asked about the baby? Every article we found talked about firefighters finding the infant beneath the tree." Avery asked.

"Someone said she had been taken to live with family by child protective services. Perhaps that rumor was started on purpose." Aunt Martha looked at Avery with one eyebrow cocked. Had she known? Was she avoiding the wrath of whoever was behind this as well?

Avery frowned. "What I don't understand is why no one ever talks about it. If there are rumors, why haven't we ever heard them?"

"You mean like the rumors the officer mentioned to you?" Brynn wrinkled her nose.

Aunt Martha did look surprised now. "What do you mean?"

Avery explained about Officer Adams bringing up rumors and failing to answer Avery's inquiries about them. "He wasn't too willing to talk."

"As if it could get him into trouble to do so?"

Aunt Martha nodded, seeming to confirm the response to her own question.

"Yes, exactly. I have my suspicions that there are things people won't say to protect themselves. And knowing most of my family is in law enforcement of some kind probably makes them extra careful around all of us." Avery pressed his lips together. "I think Officer Adams regretted mentioning it once he thought about what he said."

"So then how do we learn what these rumors might be?" Brynn wasn't going to be dissuaded so easily.

"We listen to what *isn't* being said. Right now, that's the best we can do."

It was late afternoon when they returned to Camille's, and they spent several more hours looking into the Carringtons' past. It remained quiet for the rest of the evening and Brynn's exhaustion was almost palpable.

By the time she made it into her cozy pajamas and climbed into the sweet-smelling covers, relief filled her that she could relax at last. Aunt Martha had insisted she could probably find out the attorney in charge of the Carringtons' estate. Avery had cautioned her to be very careful. The last thing they wanted to do was put her in danger.

The events of the last several hours had made her begin to question the wisdom of trying to unravel this mystery. But the assurance that she would be both giving the perpetrator what he wanted and missing out on a fascinating mystery made her dismiss any thoughts of giving up. And, regardless, she wanted to know where she came from.

A fire. A baby rescued. A strange key attached to her baby carrier, hidden under the cloth cover.

It was an odd coincidence, Brynn thought, considering she had always had a bit of a fascination with fires. But even when she had written a school paper on the science of different types of fires, no one had given any indication that she had survived one as an infant. Was that what Avery had meant when he'd talked of listening to what was not being said?

She must have drifted off at some point thinking about it, for when a knock came at her door, she was surprised to open her eyes to the early-morning light coming through her window. It took her a moment to get her bearings, but when the memory hit her, soreness from the attack two days prior did as well. Trying to get out of the comfy bed proved to be a challenge.

The knock sounded again, followed by Avery's anxious voice. "Brynn? Are you okay?"

She grabbed a robe and wrapped it around her pajamas. "Yes. I'm coming. Just a minute."

"Meet me downstairs when you're ready. I have some things to update you on," Avery called through the door, his voice sounding relieved.

Brynn hurried to brush her teeth and dress, trying not to be self-conscious about her hair, still messy after a hurried brushing. Curiosity about what Avery wanted to talk to her about overrode her other concerns.

She found Avery waiting in the breakfast nook, and Camille pouring coffee into two waiting mugs. The cozy scene sent a warm feeling over Brynn that she immediately tried to shake off.

"Good morning." Brynn aimed the greeting at them both.

Camille turned with a smile. "Good morning. How do you like your coffee?"

Brynn accepted the floral mug Camille presented to her, expression grateful. "Just a little cream. Thank you."

Camille added a bit of the thick liquid to Brynn's mug as she held it out, offering her a spoon when she had set the creamer down once more. "I'll just leave you two to talk privately. There will be bacon and waffles in a few minutes."

"That sounds delicious." Brynn smiled.

Avery merely nodded. He seemed to be all seriousness and business this morning. She took a sip of the steaming coffee and waited, watching him over the top of the mug.

He set his own cup down. "I did a little more digging last night after you went to bed."

Brynn blinked at him in surprise. She had thought he turned in for the night right after she did. "And did you find anything else?"

"I've learned some interesting things about Suzanne Davis." He frowned. "Why she came after you and threatened you, I'm not sure. But I do know she has a criminal record. She was incarcerated on charges including fraud and embezzlement just months after your adoption would have taken place. However, she somehow got released early on parole and all charges were later overturned."

"I wonder if that was somehow tied to my adoption? Do you suppose my birth parents knew her? Could they have somehow been involved with getting her convicted? Or worse, involved in her schemes?" Brynn hated to think her birth parents had been dishonest, but really, she didn't know anything about them.

Avery shook his head. "Your birth parents were honest people, Brynn. We found plenty of evidence of that looking into their backgrounds.

Your aunt said so as well. Your mother and father were both lawyers and they rallied for a lot of good changes in political circles. They were involved in their church also. It seems they were at odds with something shady going on. I can't prove it yet, but I think they might have played a part in an investigation as well."

"What makes you say that?" Brynn absently studied her right thumb as it stroked the handle of her mug. She hoped he was right about her birth parents, but she was a bit skeptical considering all she had discovered so far. A mysterious fire, a sketchy adoption agency and someone trying to keep her from learning details about her birth didn't exactly add up to a happy story.

"I grew curious about what could've led to the house fire that killed your birth parents. It said the house was a new construction, so it seems unlikely it was electrical wiring or anything of the sort. But if they were involved in some type of investigation, it might have angered someone, which could explain the house fire. The killer would've wanted to destroy any evidence they might have in the house." Avery finally paused, giving her a sympathetic look.

Brynn sucked in a breath. "Wow. My birth parents might've been working as spies?"

"I don't know about that, but they might've

known something. Are you up for a trip to Cheyenne?" Avery paused, catching a whiff of Camille's fabulous cooking. "After waffles, of course."

Brynn nodded and smiled. "I wouldn't miss the waffles."

As the smoked hickory scent of bacon filled the air, Camille stuck her head around the corner of the sectioned-off kitchen to tell them breakfast was ready. Belgian waffles, fresh strawberries, whipped cream and warm maple syrup completed the buffet table she had set up, and Brynn's mouth watered when she entered the kitchen.

Camille shooed them out as soon as they had eaten, telling them to get on with their plans for the day while she cleaned up. Brynn was sure Camille knew what Brynn and Avery were up to, but she didn't ask any questions. She no doubt heard plenty of gossip both within and outside the walls of her establishment.

The morning was cloudy and misty but still mild as Brynn followed Avery to his truck, her handbag slung over her shoulder. He reached the truck first, but before he could open the door to help Brynn inside, a bullet slammed into the side of the vehicle.

Before Brynn could react, Avery had pulled her to the ground. "Get under the truck."

Another bullet hammered the truck as he spoke.

Brynn scrambled under the truck and lay still. More shots came in a steady barrage as Avery took shelter as well. He worked his phone out of his back pocket while shielding Brynn from the shots. She concentrated on trying to breathe.

The shots continued as Brynn tried to make herself as small as possible. It wasn't an ideal hiding place. Thoughts of what might happen if a bullet struck something flammable, like a gas tank or something, sent her anxiety skyrocketing. She realized she was clenching her fists.

Brynn listened in as he called 911 and words like "active shooter" and "taking fire" made her blood go cold. He requested police help and calmly gave their location.

When he disconnected, he filled her in. "Camille called it in as well. She heard the gunshots and got to the phone about the same time I did."

Brynn's sharp intake of breath echoed under the truck's chassis. "I'm glad she's safe inside."

"Me, too. The dispatcher promised an officer in three to four minutes." Avery belly-crawled forward a few inches and peered out from under the truck. "The shots have stopped. He's probably loading a new clip. I still see his shadow, though. I'm going to try to get into the truck from the far side. I have a 9mm there, in the console."

Brynn's heart jumped up in her throat. "Be careful."

He scooted past her and out from under the truck on the driver's side, away from the shooter. He had the door open in a flash and was ducking into the cab. Once he had retrieved the weapon, he used the truck as a shield and began to return fire. She could see his feet braced behind the front tire.

Three to four minutes. Why did that sound as bad as if he had said hours instead? She reminded herself to keep breathing. In and out. *Don't think about the shooter.* She tried silently counting away the seconds. Her heartbeat pounded in her ears.

"Brynn, get in the truck on this side, but stay low." Avery called out the words to her, never shifting his stance. It brought her back into the moment. The shooter was still silent. Were they giving up?

Brynn did as Avery asked, but she didn't quite make it before the shots resumed. She shrieked and dove into the floorboard. The sound of the bullets hitting the truck and Avery firing back from just outside made her heart pound. She prayed silently, lips barely moving as she squeezed her eyes tight. Avery was risking his very life for her right now. The least she could do was pray.

She kept making petitions to the Almighty, jumping when an occasional bullet hit the truck frame a little too close to her position in the cab. Her breathing was fast, and her skin felt stretched too tightly. Worry for Avery, exposed with only the truck for minor cover, made her even more jittery.

She wasn't certain how long she stayed that way, but it seemed longer than four minutes before she heard sirens. She had lost count of the seconds long ago.

The shots stopped, but she stayed where she was for a moment, thinking Avery would surely let her know when it was clear.

But the sirens drew closer and nothing else stirred. It was too quiet. Shouldn't Avery have said something by now? Fear quickened her breathing. Seconds ticked by in silence. She finally lifted her head to take a peek.

She couldn't see Avery.

She knew he hadn't left her. Why couldn't she see him? Cautiously, she eased the door open to look around, keeping her head low as she scanned her surroundings. A patrol car was approaching, lights flashing, just yards away by the time she spotted Avery.

He was on the ground near the tire, clutching his left shoulder. His breathing was rapid and blood seeped between his fingers. She tumbled out of the truck toward him, her eyes meeting his as he spoke the obvious.

"Brynn. I'm hit."

SIX

Avery watched Brynn's face lose all color. He wanted to reassure her, but at the moment, he didn't have the strength to do more than fight to stay alert. He was dangerously close to passing out. He wasn't about to let that happen.

But she surprised him.

"Okay. Just stay still." Brynn bent over him, checking out his wound. She frowned in concentration.

At least he thought she did. Her face was getting blurry.

"Breathe, Avery. Deep breaths. Nice and slow. I'm going to flag down one of the officers and see if I can find something in your truck to staunch the blood flow." She rose from her crouched position beside him and peered over the hood of the truck. She could see the shooter disappearing into the trees.

Once she had a man radioing for paramedics, she returned to his side with an old work shirt he had tossed in the back after helping his brother Beau on the ranch last week. "You're looking really pale. Let me hold pressure for you to try and stop the blood."

He released his grip on the shoulder and re-laxed against the truck tire as she took over. The wheels dug into his back, but he hardly noticed with the raging fire in his shoulder. He just tried to focus on breathing.

An officer came over while Brynn was tying the shirt around him as a makeshift bandage. "We trailed him as long as we could, but he slipped away. Did either of you get a good look at him?"

Brynn shook her head as a paramedic took over Avery's care. "We couldn't make out any more than his shadow."

He tried to shake his head, but no one noticed. They were focused elsewhere.

"I was afraid of that. The shooter did leave some bullet casings. We're taking them for evidence. Maybe ballistics can help lead us to his identity." The officer asked a few more questions and Brynn explained about the previous attacks. Avery listened as well as he could, but he was feeling drowsier by the second.

Brynn laid a hand on his unbandaged arm. "The paramedics will get you feeling better soon."

He thought he nodded but wasn't sure. Two guys moved in, and Avery soon found himself on a gurney in the back of an ambulance. He wanted to fight to get up. Someone had to look out for Brynn. He couldn't fail her. He tried to tell the paramedics as much, but he didn't have the strength to do either. He tried to get the words out, but they came out as little more than a moaned mumble.

"Take it easy. You're going to at least need that hole stitched." The paramedic made a face at him, his expression incredulous. "I'm impressed that you're still conscious."

"Barely." Avery mumbled the word. It was almost unintelligible.

"I'm going to give you some pain medication that will probably take care of that." He held up a syringe.

"Fine." Avery didn't have an argument left.

The sun had moved a fair distance across the sky by the time he was fully conscious again, indicating it was afternoon. Brynn was hovering beside him in a hospital room. Relief almost swallowed him whole when he saw her safe.

"Hey." He was just trying to get her attention, but it sounded like a teenage boy who didn't know what to say to a girl.

She giggled. "Hi."

He tried to laugh, too. "Sorry. That sounded silly."

So did he. His voice was raw and weak.

"How are you feeling?" She scooted closer and looked him over.

"Sore. Is it stitched up?" He tried to raise himself up and look.

She nodded as she spoke, gently pushing him back down. "Stay put. The doctor said you should be careful not to break open the sutures."

He lay back against the pillow. "Ugh. For how long? I'm not much help to you like this."

He wasn't sure he was much good to her anyway. How many times now had he almost let her get shot?

"I don't know. But you've already been a really big help. And the doctor says you should be able to go home in a few hours." She glanced again at his shoulder, now professionally bandaged by hospital staff, he noticed.

"You'll be fine soon, I'm sure. You're a Thorpe. And I'm not giving up so easily. Surely there's someone around here who knows the whole story. Someone knows the truth. If I can't get it from Suzanne Davis, I'll find another way." Brynn's stubborn expression worried Avery. She was becoming frighteningly obsessed with figuring this out. It could make her careless if she continued on this path.

That would make his job of protecting her that much harder.

"We'll find the truth. But you might have to be patient. There are proven ways of finding information. I'm asking you to trust me. If you push too hard, you risk being shut down." Avery wanted to clasp her hand, to comfort her. But he didn't think that would be the right move just then. They still had to maintain some distance.

She finally nodded. After searching his face for a long moment, her hands twisted in front of her. She sounded a little hoarse when she finally spoke. "I trust you."

She didn't say any more, and he hoped she was considering what he had said. Keeping her safe was the most important thing. Solving the greatest mystery in the world would never be worth chancing her life.

It was growing late by the time Brynn got the okay to drive Avery home from the hospital. The cloudy sky was growing dark earlier than usual, and she battled a decent amount of fear as she went to get the car Camille had loaned her to bring Avery back. It would make them harder to spot, since Brynn's car was obviously being watched. Aside from that, Avery's truck had taken quite a bit of damage and needed repairs; besides, it wouldn't be so easy to get him up into the cab of the four-wheel drive.

She asked a security guard to accompany her into the parking lot. He had simply nodded, not asking for an explanation. She supposed he was likely used to females being a little frightened of making a long trek to their car alone.

She thanked him as she got into the car, and he replied with a gracious remark about doing his job before walking back to his station near the door. Brynn locked the doors and released a sigh of relief.

She thought about her earlier conversation with Avery. She had told him she trusted him, and it was true. How could she not? He had risked his life for her. Avery was a good man. She knew that. But did it mean she could trust him with her heart as well as her life?

At the covered portico, a nurse waited with Avery in a wheelchair as she drove up, his face clearly conveying his irritation. Brynn got out laughing to help him into the car.

"It's not funny. She refused to let me walk." He jerked a thumb at the nurse, who wore a slightly amused expression herself.

"Hospital policy." The nurse barked out the words. "The only other option is to stay overnight with us."

Avery grunted. "No thanks."

Both women laughed, making him scowl that much harder.

Once he was loaded into the car and they got underway, Brynn gripped the steering wheel tightly. She watched her mirrors, kept the radio turned down, and stayed alert to any suspicious activity.

"You can relax. I doubt they'd know you in Camille's car." Avery wasn't blind to her nervousness.

"Unless they're watching. They probably knew you were hit, and we had taken you to the hospital. They could've been watching for your release." Brynn pointed out the obvious. She had a feeling he just wanted to help her stay calm. She was trying, but her tension wouldn't be so easily dismissed.

Avery said nothing for a long time, making her think he agreed with her. She finally glanced over at him.

"Do you know how to shoot, Brynn?" he asked quietly.

She hesitated. "No, not really. My friends and I discussed taking a concealed carry class back in Texas, but we just never got around to it."

He nodded. "I'd like to teach you. Just to be on the safe side. We don't have time for a formal class, but I can teach you the basics."

"Is that necessary? I don't know much about

guns." She glanced his way once more and found him studying her.

"I think it's a good idea. With my injury, it could definitely be beneficial to have you know how to shoot." Avery took a wry look at his bandages.

She hesitated. "I suppose I would feel better if I at least knew how."

"I'd feel better, too. Care to start tonight?" He looked at his own rearview mirror.

"As soon as we get back?" She thought he meant to work on it at Camille's place.

"I was actually going to suggest we drive out to the firing range before we went back to Camille's. It's not far." Avery pulled up a map on his phone with his good hand.

Brynn felt nervousness bubble up within her at the thought, but she decided it would be worth conquering her fears. This was one thing she could have control over. "Fine. Just give me directions."

They reached the gun range and Avery led her inside. The man working eyed him speculatively, taking in his bandaged shoulder and raising an eyebrow.

"Don't worry. She's the one doing the shooting today." Avery made the quip with a gesture to Brynn standing behind him.

"I'll need ID and some paperwork." The man

instructed them on what he needed them to do, and Brynn complied with a nervous nod. Before she knew what was happening, she had a handgun clutched carefully in her grip and Avery was instructing her on how to hit the target.

Brynn winced as Avery handed her the Glock. It felt too heavy and clumsy in her grip. He smiled, though, and began to teach her the workings of the weapon. He explained how to load the clip how to aim, and reassured her that he would be right there with her the whole time.

He showed her how to stand properly before letting her fire. Her stance was awkward at first, but she finally got it. Getting everything down correctly took her some time, much longer than she expected. The gun felt unnatural in her hands and the slight kick was hard to get used to. Avery talked her through it patiently, however, and once she learned how to cup her left hand under her right and steady the trigger hand, she was hitting it quite consistently near the bull's-eye. Avery gently encouraged her at every turn, and she found her nerves fading under the warmth of his grin.

"You're a natural." He finally eased the gun from her hand. "I think you're ready to defend yourself if need be."

Looking at her watch, she realized they had been there well over an hour. The time had gone quickly, and she realized she had enjoyed it.

"You're a great teacher." She smiled as she replied to his words with a compliment of her own.

"Coming from a professional teacher, I appreciate that." He led the way from the room.

"Thank you, Avery." She exhaled. "For the compliment as well as for teaching me how to shoot."

"You're welcome."

His gaze was warm, and she felt a tenderness well up inside her without warning. This was the kind of thing she had to watch out for. Maybe she knew for sure that Avery wasn't married, but there was still a deep fear of her own mistakes. Avery might be worthy of her trust, but she knew he didn't want a relationship. It would be a waste of time to dream of one.

Brynn turned, hoping her expression didn't betray her emotions, and started to the car. Her thoughts were still on Avery and the unwelcome tenderness she was beginning to feel for him, however, and she didn't notice the shadow falling across the gravel parking lot until it was too late.

The chill hit her about the same time as the words.

"Come quietly and no one will get hurt."

The voice sent almost as much fear coursing through her as the nose of the gun that met her eyes when she turned.

SEVEN

Brynn hadn't seemed to notice when Avery had paused to answer a question from the man working the counter at the gun range. He had tried to get her attention, but despite the ear protection she had worn, firing the gun for so long must have affected her hearing.

Now he hurried after her, trying to dismiss his certainty that something had gone wrong.

He rushed out the door, hoping to find her walking safely to the borrowed car. Instead, his fears were realized. A man was urging her away at gunpoint toward an inconspicuous SUV sitting on the opposite side of the parking lot.

He jerked his gun from his waistband while shouting at the man. "Stop right there!"

The abductor whirled Brynn around to face Avery, the gun still pointed far too close to her head. The man wore a black face covering pulled high up on his nose, and a toboggan cap of the same shade that met it around the ears. His gun hand shook almost imperceptibly, but he jerked Brynn around to shield himself from Avery's weapon.

The look of sheer terror on Brynn's face sent Avery's adrenaline on an upward spiral. He knew he didn't have a clean shot with Brynn between them. His best bet would be to talk the man down or distract him.

"You don't wanna do this. Just let her go and you can be gone." Avery didn't waver. His gun stayed aimed just past Brynn, though he knew the shot was too risky.

"I can't let her go. She's coming with me, dead or alive. Drop your gun or it will be the first option." The gunman's voice didn't sound super confident, which led Avery to believe this situation could go badly in a hurry if he wasn't careful.

He held the gun steady for a second longer, then lowered it with a long growl of annoyance.

The man didn't respond to his statement. "Put the gun on the ground, turn around and go back inside."

Avery hesitated.

"Do it now!" The man yelled the words, voice shaking more than his hand.

One thing was clear to Avery. This man wasn't experienced at taking hostages, and maybe not even at firing a weapon. Avery could definitely use that to his advantage.

He complied, laying his weapon down and turning away from them as he started to rise. Before he did, he glanced at the man to be sure he was watching. Then he took a calculated risk.

He snatched the gun back up, and just as Avery had expected, the man turned his gun on Avery, leaving Brynn to wrest her way out of his grip. Avery rolled as the gun went off, but Brynn reacted quickly. She kneed the gunman in the groin as he tried to take aim at Avery once more. He dropped his gun and as it hit the gravel, he grasped his middle.

"Run!" Avery shouted, and Brynn took one more shot at the man, elbowing him in the nose before fleeing.

Avery didn't have time to admire her bravado, however, and rushed toward the man. He twisted the man's arm behind his back and kicked the gun away from him.

The masked man didn't give up quite so easily. He reached around with his free hand and tried to get a shot in at Avery's face with his fist. Avery ducked the punch, but the man managed to twist his arm out of Avery's grip.

Battling the searing pain in his wound, Avery lowered his shoulder and dove at the man's midsection. He drove him to the ground where they rolled a few times trying to overpower one another. Each encounter with the ground sent a new jolt of pain through his entire upper body. He countered it with a reminder that Brynn needed him.

Avery finally managed to subdue the man. He gripped the man's wrists firmly in his good hand, holding them above his head. Avery gritted his teeth, the throbbing in his shoulder making the task more difficult.

"Who are you? Who are you working for?" Avery let up pressure just enough for the man to suck in a breath. He didn't answer. He just shook his head.

"What do they want with her?" Avery pressed in on the man again, then let up enough to allow him to talk.

"I don't know. I just took the money they offered me." The man's face was red, and he was starting to look terrified. His gaze kept straying to Avery's shoulder, which he was certain was bleeding once more. He would probably need more stitches.

Avery had more important problems to solve. "Who offered you money?"

"I don't know! I just got a text. They told me where to find the first half of the money and promised to Cash App the rest to me from a business account." The man writhed, trying to get free.

"What was the name of the business account?" Avery asked. "Who was the text from?"

The man was frantically shaking his head. "I don't know, man! I swear, I don't know. It was one of those weird text numbers like you get from businesses. I was just supposed to deliver the girl."

"To whom? Where were you supposed to take her?" Avery tightened his grip on the man, and he stopped struggling.

"Some abandoned warehouse. The address is in my phone. Look, man, I was just trying to make some money. I have a family." His panic was real.

"Do you have this phone on you?" Avery held him securely, glad to hear sirens in the distance. Brynn must have called 911 once she got away.

"It's in the SUV." His face was turning purple, but Avery didn't have a lot of sympathy for the man. "Key's in my pocket."

Two squad cars entered the parking lot, their sirens giving one last whoop before going silent. Avery surrendered the captive man to one of the officers bearing cuffs and began explaining what he knew. The other officer retrieved the keys from the captive's pocket.

They found the phone, which the officer took into custody.

Avery spoke to the officer in charge for some time, answering his questions and explaining the situation. "I'd really like to know what you find on that phone. My client started having all these problems as soon as she began looking into find out who her birth parents are. We believe we know, but the circumstances are suspicious. I'm in contact with a detective in Cheyenne about it as well, but we think her birth parents were killed in a house fire. She somehow survived."

The officer went a little pale. "Wow. Really?"

Avery nodded. The officer just shook his head.

"So you'll keep me updated on your findings, Officer Blanton?"

"Of course." He hurriedly left Avery and returned to his fellow officers.

They had already loaded the handcuffed man into the patrol car and Avery stood and watched them go, trying to ignore the burning in his shoulder.

He suspected there was more going on in Laramie County than anyone knew. And he was starting to fear the cover-up might be far too big to take on alone.

As if to underscore his point, Avery's phone

began to vibrate from his back pocket. Glancing at it before accepting the call, he greeted Wilder with his last name.

"Hey, buddy, I was able to ferret out a name you might be interested in in regards to that cold case. When I started to trace back files from around the time of the house fire, I found Rebecca and Anderson Carrington were in contact with a detective over something before they died. His name was Weston Davis. I thought he might know something about why the Carringtons might have been targeted. But I have really bad news about that. He's dead."

Brynn examined Avery's stitches carefully. He had bled through his bandages, but there didn't seem to be any major damage. "I think they are all still intact, but I'm certainly no doctor. I would advise you to return to the hospital."

Avery scowled back at her. "I'm not going back."

He was still wondering how he was going to tell her what he had just learned from Wilder about the detective. It was making him cranky trying to figure it all out.

And his wound was on fire.

She didn't flinch at his sharp tone, however. "Then suffer the consequences, I suppose. I've done all I can do. If it scars badly or gets infected..."

She shrugged as if she didn't care.

Camille watched with amusement from the door to the kitchen. Avery had drawn her into the room when he had howled in agony at the antiseptic Brynn had cleaned the wound with, removing the dried blood so she could see the sutures. Camille had hurried in to see what was going on.

"I think you're putting on, anyway. You didn't put up this much fuss when you first got shot." Brynn was exhausted and frustrated, but not so much that she couldn't give some of the aggravation back to Avery that he was doling out.

"She's right, you know." Camille smiled. "What happened to that tough guy that refused to pass out with a gunshot wound to the shoulder?"

Avery just kept right on scowling at them both.

Brynn knelt next to him, handing him a pain reliever and a glass of water. "I really am grateful for you."

He shook his head, refusing the pain medication. "I need to be clearheaded. I can't take a chance of being loopy from narcotics if anything happens."

"I understand. Would you at least take an over-the-counter pain medicine? Ibuprofen or acetaminophen, maybe?" Brynn frowned at him but put the high-powered pain pills back in the prescription container from the hospital.

He grunted his consent.

Camille disappeared up the stairs and in the silence, Avery knew he had to tell Brynn.

"Wilder called back about the cases we had him looking into. It seems the Carringtons were in contact with a detective by the name of Weston Davis." He wasn't eager to proceed.

"And?" Brynn's brow wrinkled.

"And he died a few months ago. They ruled it a suicide." Avery hated having to tell her this. Her kind-hearted nature was taking a beating for sure.

"That's terrible. Do you think that's really what happened?" Her expressive eyes glowed with sympathy.

He gave her an incredulous look. "Of course not. But I can't prove it."

"Did his family believe it?" Brynn looked up at Camille as she reentered the room.

Avery, too, looked her way. "I don't know. But I'd like to find out. He had a young wife, a small child and a sister. Surely one of them would have known if he was that depressed."

"Could we talk to them?" Brynn asked.

"I have Wilder looking into it. He's also look-ing into other fires in the area from the past couple of decades. I think there might be a connection." Avery rose to walk down the hall.

Before he could get far, however, Camille drew their attention to the window. Someone had pulled into the driveway. "The county sheriff is here."

Avery turned and came closer to look. Camille met the sheriff at the door and invited him in. He took one look at Avery's shoulder and grimaced. "It's worse than I thought."

"Good to see you too, Nick." Avery groused. "When did they get so desperate for a sheriff?"

Nick Sheffield had come to Wyoming from Texas when Avery was a senior in high school. They had become friends quickly, and Nick had spent summers working on the Thorpe family ranch for a while when Avery still lived at home.

Nick chuckled good-naturedly. "I'm still not sure how I got elected."

"Me, either." Avery rolled his eyes. But it was a bit of a mystery. People around here didn't usually want what they considered outsiders in positions of power. But the Sheffield family had been well-respected.

Brynn looked from one man to the other, unsure what was happening between the two men. To her surprise, Nick laughed and clapped Avery on the good shoulder. "You Thorpe boys have always been talented at finding trouble. It's a wonder you all ended up in law enforcement and military."

Avery's mouth quirked up on one side as he thought of the many scrapes he had gotten into with his daredevil brothers. They were fearless to a fault. "I guess you're right."

At Brynn's questioning glance, he explained. "You remember my four brothers, right? Always stirring something up around town or at the ranch. The church ladies in town just shook their heads and said it was because we had been left without a mother in the home."

He said it in a joking tone, but it had honestly taken Avery a while to forgive his mother for leaving him and his brothers when they were younger. It wasn't until Grayson married Lauren that the family had reconciled. It was too late for his father, however, who had passed away a few years prior to that.

Brynn nodded. "I heard they've excelled as Special Forces and such. And then Grayson, the former US marshal, working as an advisor for White House security now. What about Caldwell, though? I haven't heard much about him."

Avery's expression darkened. He didn't want to talk about Caldwell. Their dissension weighed on him. "He's a lawyer in Texas. Last I knew working for the Texas State Bureau of Investigation."

She must have read his expression; she let it drop with a quick acknowledgment. "Oh, I see."

Avery refocused his attention on Nick. "Are you here to help, or just cause more trouble?"

Nick's expression sobered. "I'll help if I can. Fill me in on the details."

Avery did so, with Brynn making an occasional comment. Camille was in and out, bringing drinks and a tray of cheeses and crackers, ever the gracious hostess.

"We didn't learn much from the phone. It was a burner, and all we got was an obscure business named DSP Merchandising. The address listed for it is an abandoned lot where an old warehouse burned down five years ago." Nick rattled off the information with a wry expression.

"My best guess," Nick continued, "is the guy knew someone who told your kidnapper how to make a little extra money. Looks like he contacted the business number first."

"He's no professional." Avery snorted. "Any luck learning who he is?

"We're trying to get a positive ID on him. He was carrying false identification. He might not be a professional, but whoever hired him could be. Someone hooked him up with them." Nick shrugged.

"Sounds about right. He has to know someone who knows something. I'll check out every possible connection to Suzanne Davis." Avery returned his frown. "I'm also looking into someone who likes to start fires. Know anyone with that MO?"

Nick's expression took on a serious cast. "Not right off, but I'll check into it. But the first thing I'm going to recommend is to get her out of this town. I can't say a lot, but I can tell you I wouldn't feel right about keeping her here."

"Where would we go?" Avery was shaking his head.

"Does she have any relatives or anything somewhere away from here?" Nick glanced at Brynn.

"We need to be careful not to put anyone else in danger." Avery reminded them.

"Could Grayson set you up with a safe house somewhere nearby?" Nick knew Grayson still had connections in the marshals service.

"Maybe so. I'll see what he can do." Avery began tapping on his phone.

Soon after, the details had all been worked out. They wouldn't have to go far. The house was about twenty or thirty minutes away.

They finalized all the needed arrangements, and Brynn and Avery began to pack up to head out of town.

Avery's truck was still being repaired, so after thanking Camille, they piled their bags into the trunk and got into Brynn's car.

"We'll drive through town, stop for fuel and do our best to be seen. I'm sure someone is keeping watch anyway." Avery was behind the wheel in case they needed to lose a tail. He was more experienced at defensive driving and Brynn didn't want the responsibility of shaking off a pursuer.

Brynn shivered involuntarily. She didn't like the thought of someone watching her every move, but she knew Avery was probably right. "You really think we'll be able to lose them once we get out of town? Maybe my leaving town will be enough to end the threat."

"I suspect it's gone too far for that. And they did follow you here. Our best chance is to figure out who's behind it. Obviously there's someone more powerful behind Ms. Davis calling the shots. Didn't she say as much outside the diner that night?" Avery peered through the windshield.

"Yes, but can we trust what she says? She pulled a knife on me." Brynn huffed out a breath.

"I don't think she'd lie about that. This is bigger than some crumbling old adoption agency." Avery pulled into a busy gas station in the middle of town.

Brynn looked around the station watching for anything suspicious. "Nothing else from your friend Wilder lately?"

He shifted the car into Park. "Not since we heard about Weston Davis. We'll get in touch with him once we get settled."

Brynn acknowledged his words with a nod as he got out to pump the gas. He used a card to pay at the pump so he wouldn't have to leave her side, and she did her best not to watch him, but he kept drawing her gaze. She had never known any man so good.

A bird flitted out from under the portico cover of the station, startling her. She gave herself a little shake for being so jumpy. This was a highly visible station in the middle of town. Avery was keeping watch. She was safe.

But the feeling of anxiousness lingered.

As they began to drive toward the exit, however, she noticed a dark van driving in. The driver had a ball cap pulled low over his eyes, and a thick beard below his nose. Brynn watched in the rearview mirror as he pulled into a parking space. She continued to watch while they pulled away, but no one got out of the van.

"Avery, the van." She turned in her seat. "I think he was watching us. No one ever got out."

"Are you sure? He just pulled in. Maybe it's

just taking him a minute." Avery glanced in his own mirrors.

"I'll keep watch, but he'll be out of sight soon." She turned a little more.

They both fell silent as Avery drove. Brynn finally lost sight of the van and turned back to settle into the passenger seat. An upbeat country song played softly on the radio and the late-afternoon sky was growing dark. The cloud cover deepened the sky into an intense gray and drops of rain began to pepper the windshield.

It wasn't five minutes later that a shadowy dark vehicle appeared in the rearview mirrors. It was distant, but a shiver shook through Brynn, nonetheless.

"Can you tell if it's the same van?" Avery asked the question as Brynn turned again in her seat.

She tugged at her seat belt strap. "Not yet."

Avery's attention darted between the rearview mirror and the rain-speckled front windshield. "It's getting closer."

Brynn made a sound of agreement. "It's a dark blue van."

"That can't be a coincidence." Avery stepped on the gas. "Time to lose him."

The little Mazda shot forward. The van followed suit.

"There. Take that side road." Brynn pointed up ahead. "It's gravel. He'll have to slow down."

Avery did as she suggested. The Mazda peeled out a little on the rocks as he turned, but still accelerated. The van followed, fishtailing a bit into the turn.

"He's still on us. He's catching up." Brynn couldn't keep the panic from her voice.

Thunder rumbled ominously and lightning flared in the distance. It glowed off the sleek sides of the dark van and outlined it in light.

The van driver sped up again and swerved over, coming along beside them.

In response, Avery hit the brakes, probably thinking their pursuer would fly on past them. Instead, the van jerked hard right and clipped the front of the car. When Avery braked harder to avoid the van, the loose gravel sent the car into a fishtail.

Brynn could only hang on tight as they spun right into the deep culvert alongside the road.

EIGHT

Gravel and mud flew around them as the Mazda spun to a stop. The car leaned heavily toward the ditch, pitching Avery and Brynn forward into their seat belts and toward the dash.

But Avery's concern was on the van. He could barely see it in his outside rearview mirror. It had come to a sliding halt and was now backing toward them at a crazy speed, weaving back and forth across the road. Brake lights flared just as the nose of a gun appeared out the driver's-side window.

Brynn said his name, panic edging her voice.

"Get down. I'm gonna get us out of here." Avery tried to reverse, but the tires only spun. Putting it in Drive, he plunged them further into the ditch. He held his breath as he punched it. The tires alternately spun and caught. They inched forward as a bullet struck the dirt just in front of the passenger door. The tires spun and caught again. Finally, they shot forward, and as the car climbed out the other side of the ditch, Avery wheeled it around.

"Hold on. It's gonna be rough." Avery squinted and gripped the wheel as he drove back across the deep ditch and into the road. The bouncing jarred their teeth as they shot over the rutted ditch. Another shot kicked up dirt and gravel a little too close as they picked up speed.

The car fishtailed as Avery guided it back onto the dirt road. He could hear the pop of the pistol from the man still firing off a couple of shots behind them. The shots stopped just before he noted the van turning around to follow from the view in his mirrors.

Brynn was still crouched down in the floorboard, and she looked up at him. "Is it safe to get up?"

He didn't answer right away. "I think so. He's still turning around. I'm going to take some turns and try to lose him."

Brynn scrambled back up into the seat and refastened her seat belt. Then she craned her neck around to watch the van. "He's coming. Hurry!"

"There're a lot of trees on one of the side roads up ahead. I'm going to try to get up there and see if I can stay hidden long enough to lose him." Avery sped up as much as he dared on the gravel road. But another vehicle appeared in the distance, coming at them from the other direction.

"Uh-oh." Brynn gasped. "Looks like he might have help."

The same sedan that had followed Brynn from the adoption house was barreling toward them. Avery spoke his thoughts aloud. "I think they plan to hit us head-on."

He regretted the admission as soon as the words were out. Brynn's fear was almost palpable. "What're you going to do? There's nowhere else to turn and if you stop, the van will ram into us."

Avery eyed his surroundings. If the car hit them head-on, they would be crushed between it and the van behind them. But if he hit the ditch at this speed, he would likely lose control and flip. If he tried to swerve around them at the last minute, they could still fishtail and end up in the ditch.

But there was a chance the other two vehicles would collide, disabling the drivers enough to make them give up the chase.

He glanced at Brynn, white with terror. He would have to take the risk.

"Brace yourself. I'm going to slow just a little and try to swerve around them at the last second. It might not end well. But I think it's our best shot." Avery looked at his knuckles, white with his concentrated grip.

"I trust you." Brynn's head bobbed her confirmation.

He looked at her questioningly once more, making sure she was okay with his decision, then nodded back at her. "Okay."

He had to time this out just right. He couldn't even flinch too early or the driver of the car would realize his intent and swerve as well. But if he waited too long...

Adrenaline rushed through him. The rain had almost stopped, now barely a drizzle, and though there were a few muddy places, the road wasn't packed down very tightly. There would be enough loose dirt and gravel to cause him to skid. And if the other vehicles reacted, they could all slide into a pile-up.

Would they guess his plan? He sucked in a breath. He waited, held steady, and at just the right second, he braked and pulled the steering wheel hard enough to miss the oncoming vehicle. For a split second, the edge of the road near the ditch grabbed at his tires and threatened to tug him on over into it. He fought for control and managed to regain the roadway just as the other two vehicles skidded, swerved and sideswiped each other. The vehicles spun and skittered in response, a picture of ugly chaos, and

Avery watched from the rearview mirror as he accelerated once more.

Avery heard Brynn let out a relieved breath. The two other vehicles shook to a halt, and they could see that neither the sedan nor the van had incurred a great deal of damage. The sedan recovered more quickly than the van, whose tires spun in the gravel trying to regain purchase with the weight imbalance where it tipped into the ditch.

The sound of crunching gravel told him one of the vehicles had begun to pursue them once more. Brynn confirmed it. "We still haven't lost them. The sedan is following."

Avery glanced at his mirror for confirmation. "We will. I'm going to take a turn up here that might help."

Brynn was grateful Avery knew the area so well. She couldn't see a turn ahead, but there was a stand of trees that would likely do a pretty good job of concealing it in the deepening late-afternoon gloom. The question would be whether or not the driver of the sedan was familiar with the area.

The rain picked up its tempo once again, pummeling the car with heavy drops and making Avery slow the car down to gain better visibility of the road.

"Wow. This downpour is intense." Brynn

tried to make out their tail. "But the good news is, I can't see the other car. Maybe they can't see us, either."

"Well, that's a small blessing. But my brake lights will flare when I slow down to turn. Maybe I should go straight a little further to see if we can lose them." Avery spoke his thoughts aloud.

"Do you think the driver might be fooled if you braked, but kept going? It's hard to see much in this heavy rain." Brynn's face seemed to say she wasn't sure it would work.

"It's worth a try." Avery looked down at his phone. "We're going to have to find a way to shake them off."

He came to the intersection, braked as she had suggested, then drove on very slowly, hoping to see if the car followed. It was dangerous to be out here driving without headlights in this downpour, but he didn't know how else to stay hidden from the car pursuing them.

"At the next intersection, I'll turn. I'll just go slow enough to not have to hit my brakes so the lights won't give us away." Avery kept up a steady speed and then eased off the gas to let the car slow as another turnoff came into view. He could barely make it out in the rain-drenched light. He made the turn, Brynn watching to see

if she could make out their tail anywhere behind them.

"I don't see anyone." She leaned hard, straining to see. "Maybe we are in the clear."

He hoped she was right. But his instincts told
him this wasn't over yet.

Brynn wanted nothing more than to get away
from these people and get to the safe house for
the night. They had just turned back onto a
paved road once more, but they were still having to creep along in the rain. It was so frus-
trating. She was worn out from the adrenaline,
and she knew Avery had to be tired, too, though
he seemed to be taking it very well. He seemed
alert and relaxed, while she felt both tired and
overstimulated. It was like wanting to go to
sleep after drinking way too much coffee.

Avery must have realized her plight, because
he glanced at her and shook his head. "You don't
have to keep watch right now. I can see almost
as well in my mirrors. There's no need for you
to keep straining your neck."

She smiled at him. "I appreciate that. But I
need something to keep myself occupied."

"I understand that." He glanced over his
shoulder. "Actually, maybe you can help with
something else. My laptop is in the case behind
the seat. You could get it out and see if Wilder

has sent me any more information. My phone is wedged in my pocket right now. Using the laptop would be easier. If he could get us those files from the Carringtons' house fire, it might give us some leads."

Brynn did as he said, entering the login information he gave her carefully. She realized it was no small thing that he was trusting her with this, and it sent a warm feeling through her at the thought. She quickly dismissed it, however. No more romantic entanglements. She was content alone.

She forced her mind back to the task at hand. She pulled up the email inbox as he directed. "Okay, got it."

"Look for anything from Wilder Hawthorne. He should have sent it sometime today. After I texted him to tell him about what happened he said he would email me later." Avery was looking in the mirrors again. "I'm going to have to turn on my headlights. It's almost completely dark."

In that instant, more headlights appeared. It sent Brynn's adrenaline soaring again. "Is it them?"

"I can't tell in the dark." Avery sounded frustrated.

Brynn didn't know where to focus. Finally, she decided to examine the emails as she had been trying to do before. She scanned through them once. Twice. A third time, with the same result. "Avery, there isn't an email from Wilder Hawthorne. Are you sure he was going to send it today?"

The lights inched closer, but she tried not to dwell on it. Avery seemed preoccupied by them as well.

"Yes, I'm positive. He told me twice that he would. And Wilder has never let me down." Worry colored Avery's face at this statement.

"You think something happened? Or maybe he's just still trying to track down the files from the case?" Brynn felt a knot of concern form in her midsection. Was her need to know what had happened to her birth parents endangering other people? What if they had caught on to Avery's friend? Maybe they'd figured out he was helping her and decided to put a stop to it.

Avery must have guessed what was on her mind. "I'll call him as soon as we get to the safe house. Try not to worry. I'm sure it's just a fluke."

Brynn wasn't convinced, but she didn't say any more about it. She didn't have a chance.

The headlights behind them suddenly sped closer. "Avery, I think it's the van. How did he find us again?"

Avery also accelerated as much as he dared

in the rainy conditions. "I don't know. Maybe he got lucky. Maybe he's tracking us somehow."

"He just keeps getting closer. What can we do?" Brynn heard the pitch increase in her own voice. Her stomach rolled and she felt sick.

He didn't answer right away. He kept both hands on the wheel, and the water collecting on the roadway tugged at them every so often, slowing the car as it threw up torrents of water along the sides. The dirt along the ditches had turned to soggy muck and sucked at the tires.

"He's trying to force us into going too fast in this weather, hoping we will wreck." Avery explained the man's tactics.

"What if you slow down?" Brynn was afraid of the answer.

"I think he'll run into us and try to force us into a wreck anyway. He seems pretty desperate to get the job done." Avery shook his head as if it was no good. He pushed down on the gas again, testing his limits.

The van sped closer as well. The headlights seemed only inches from their bumper.

"Hold on. I'm going to turn toward town. Hopefully once we get to a more populated area he'll think twice about harassing us anymore." He squinted a bit as he slowed to turn, his expression indicating he hoped the van didn't do anything stupid.

No collision came, though the van followed. The rain picked up again as well. Where was all the other traffic that should be on the road? It wasn't that late. Why was this area so deserted?

Just as Avery thought they might have lost the van, it suddenly came racing up alongside them. The driver of the sedan must have jumped into the van after their collision. He saw the pistol jutting out of the open passenger-side window just in time to tell Brynn to get down.

The shots fired at close range, and Avery slammed on the brakes, hoping to make the shooter miss, but the wet pavement sent them into a skid. Brynn screamed as the Mazda spun once more, this time catching on a culvert beside the road and hurtling them end over end. The world went topsy-turvy before finally settling them upright once again. Avery felt his stomach flip along with the car. They came to rest at an odd angle to the road, headlights glaring out into an open field. A shaking rocked them clumsily as the car shuddered to a standstill. Torrents of rain sluiced across the arc of light, but Avery couldn't make out a whole lot through the shattered windshield. The side windows were also destroyed, and the outside rearview mirror on the driver's side hung limply from the frame.

Haziness corrupted his thoughts for a moment, until finally the present became clear.

Fear flooded him like the pounding rain filling the road.

"Brynn." She hadn't been fastened in, having unbuckled her seatbelt to reach for the laptop. He was thankful she hadn't been thrown from the vehicle.

She didn't answer. He leaned over the console to get a closer check on her unconscious form. He checked her pulse. He breathed a sigh of relief to find it steady and strong. A knot on her temple foretold a likely concussion, however. She needed an ambulance.

He wasn't sure if he should move her, but the van was coming back. If he didn't get her out of here, they would be an easy target. The first responder training he had received in his early days before becoming a cop served him well, though. He checked all her limbs quickly, examined her trunk, and as he was finishing, she began to moan.

"Can you hear me? We have to get out of here. They're coming back. Do you hurt anywhere besides your head?" Avery spoke to her gently, but insistently. He really needed her to respond. If he couldn't get her out of here soon, they were as good as dead.

"Hmm." Brynn turned her head from side to side. That was a good sign. No neck injuries.

"I'm going to pull you out and put you on my back. Do you understand what I'm saying?" Avery was hoping the more he talked to her, the more alert she would remain. He reached for his door handle.

It was stuck.

He tried unlocking it, but it still didn't budge. The rolling vehicle had likely jammed it into the frame. He sucked in a breath. It would be more difficult to get her out of the passenger side from where he sat, but he didn't have much choice.

Climbing over her as gently as he could in the small space, Avery pulled the door handle of the passenger side. It wasn't a very large car, and wedging his large frame into the area between Brynn and the dash wasn't easy. He prayed this door wasn't stuck as well.

Pulling the latch produced no result. With a deep breath and a grunt, he shoved at it the best he could at his cramped and twisted angle. The door gave with a groan, probably a little warped also. He tumbled out, grabbing his cell phone and shoving it quickly into his pocket, and then reached back inside to carefully tug Brynn's limp form into his arms.

The van's headlights rushed toward them. He didn't have much time.

Avery pulled Brynn over his shoulder and dashed off, away from all the headlights. It was dark and wet, and he stumbled more than once in the mud, but he ran as fast as he could. He thought they were in a field someone had started clearing for a housing development, but he couldn't be sure. He ran for the distant trees, the shadow of the mountains looming in the distance. He thought there was a small lake nearby as well, but he was still turned around a little from the rolling car.

He chanced a glimpse over his shoulder to see if the van's passengers were in pursuit. He thought he heard one of the van doors close over the sound of the deluge of rainwater, and a shadow flitted across the van's headlights. A shadowy figure moved toward the car. They must not have seen Avery pull Brynn from the car.

Good, maybe they would waste some time looking for them there.

He had to get Brynn somewhere safe and dry. He ran toward the trees, hoping there would be a house somewhere on the other side. Ignoring his boots sliding on the unstable ground, he raced toward the cover.

Brynn moaned from just behind his shoulder.

"Hang tight. I know you're hurting. I'm trying to get you somewhere safe." He spoke in broken words as he sprinted over the tufted grass around his ankles.

She made a sound he thought might be part whimper, part agreement. His chest clenched in concern.

"If we can get to the trees, maybe we can find shelter."

Rain sluiced down his face, drenching his T-shirt, and his damp jeans clung to his legs in a wet vise. He ignored all of it. The van's passengers had begun to shout, probably realizing they were fleeing on foot.

A gunshot sounded, but Avery didn't think they had spotted them. Probably just hoping to get lucky. More shouting followed, and he thought he made out a woman's voice saying something about wasting bullets.

Let them argue with one another. That might buy Brynn and himself some time as well.

The tree line was inching closer, far too slowly to suit Avery, but at last they reached it.

"There! Going into the trees!" the woman yelled.

A gunshot followed, this time just after the sound of a bullet glancing off a tree way too close to where they had just dashed into the cover of trees.

He heard the faint sound of sloshing as the couple ran toward them. Avery had to slow now because of the undergrowth. Tree roots and low-lying brush threatened to trip him, and Brynn was trying to move now, coming more alert. She made a sound of dismay as another bullet ricocheted through the trees.

"Stay still. I've got you." Avery wanted to reassure her, but there wasn't much he could do. He kept speaking to her in low tones and stumbling through the woods. Now that she was alert, he shifted her to his back, running with her piggyback-style through the woods.

More arguing behind him indicated one of the would-be assassins didn't know much about tracking. They couldn't agree on which way to go. Avery made out just enough to realize the woman was on the right track. He hoped the man wouldn't listen to her.

"Avery." Brynn whispered. "Turn to your right. Are those house lights?"

He hadn't seen the tiny twinkling through the trees. He let out a breath, still huffing from his weighted sprint across the muddy field. "You're amazing."

"Nah. I'd tell you to let me down, but I'm a little woozy." She sounded as much as she said it, her voice still a mere whisper.

"No, stay put. I don't want to take any chances."

He hurried off with her in the direction of the lights.

Their pursuers fired off another shot. Brynn bit back a little squeak, and Avery crouched as low as he could while moving forward with Brynn on his back. They seemed to be getting closer, but he wasn't sure if the duo had actually spotted them again. The heavy stand of trees hindered the rain so that Avery at least wasn't blinking it from his eyes.

The gunshots kept coming, but Avery finally crashed through the edge of the tree line and right into the backyard of a house. The rain pummeled them once more and he rushed for the patio cover behind the house. Lights were on and he thought he heard a television or a radio playing inside. He knocked on the back door.

Movement from inside let him know that someone had heard. He stood there silently praying they would open the door before their pursuers caught up to them. He settled Brynn on her feet, steadying her, while they waited.

"Do you think they'll let us in?" She whispered the question.

"I hope so."

In response, the door swung open at that moment.

And the twin barrels of a shotgun met them.

NINE

Avery had thrown his hands in the air and stepped in front of Brynn, but not before she had experienced a jolt of horror at the gun staring them in the face.

She was miserably cold and wet, and her head hurt so badly she could cry. Now they had guns aimed at them from both sides? Just when she thought they had reached safety. The injustice of it all was almost too much.

Avery was speaking calmly to the man holding the gun. "We don't mean you any harm. We've been in a car accident and just need some shelter until we can get an ambulance."

The man slowly lowered the shotgun. "Avery Thorpe?"

Brynn stood blindly behind him as he responded. "Yes. Do we know each other?"

The man set down the gun and extended his hand. "It's been a long time. Flint McElroy. I knew your father. Get inside here."

"Thank you." Avery said the words as he ushered Brynn in first.

The man looked out before closing the door. "I heard gunshots. Thought you might be bringing trouble to my stoop."

Brynn shifted uneasily, but Avery just replied with honesty. "To be honest, sir, we could be. I'd appreciate it if you kept that shotgun handy until we can get some help."

The gray-haired man's brow furrowed. "What do you mean? Someone's after you?"

In response, Avery introduced Brynn. "They're after her, actually. I'm trying to protect her. They forced us into a rollover accident. We had to flee on foot."

"That explains that goose egg. Better get her to a hospital. I can get you there faster than an ambulance." Flint frowned at the pair of them.

"I don't want to put anyone else in danger." Brynn was shaking her head.

"No worries about that." Flint winked at her. "There's a state trooper that lives across the street. He's home right now, squad car parked in the drive. But if you'd rather wait, I understand."

He gestured out the front window, but it was too far to see out in the dark and the rain. Brynn was still thankful to know there was a police unit in his neighbor's drive. "Thank goodness."

"I'll give him a call and get him over here. In

the meantime, Betsy will keep them from crossing the threshold." He picked the shotgun back up and handed it to Avery.

"We'd appreciate that, sir," Avery said.

Flint made a phone call and in seconds, the trooper had promised to head straight over.

"My wife is out with her sister this evening at some church event. But she'd have my hide if I didn't offer you some dry clothes and something to eat." Flint looked at the pair of them, soaked to the bone and trying not to drip on too much of his kitchen floor.

"Thank you, but we'd hate to inconvenience you. Some towels would be welcome, though." Avery peeked out the back window. "I'll keep watch here with Betsy."

Flint just nodded and disappeared down the hall. Brynn fought back a shiver. The damp was starting to get to her, but she knew Avery was right. They couldn't stay here long. What if the man's wife came back, unsuspecting, and walked right into danger?

About that time, a knock came at the back door.

Avery gestured at her. "Go. Out of sight. Just in case."

Brynn did as he commanded, but a few seconds later, she heard him opening the door to the trooper. "Thank you for coming over, Officer Thomas."

"Call me Ken." The man responded as they walked into the living room. "I know of your reputation. All the Thorpes, actually. Good men. I'd be honored to consider you a friend."

"Thank you, Ken." Avery gestured toward Brynn as she reappeared. "This is Brynn Evans."

"Nice to meet you," she said, teeth chattering just a bit.

Flint returned and handed them some fluffy towels. "This should help."

"There's an ambulance on the way. I called dispatch to route them here as I came over, and I scanned the area outside for your pursuers, but I didn't see anything. They must've fled back to their vehicle. Someone reported the accident, but no one was found at the scene, just a smashed-up car and an empty van. Now I know why. Tell me about what happened." Ken looked from one to the other.

Avery gave his shortened version of the tale while Brynn wrapped up and tried not to shiver. Flint looked on with interest, silent, but nodding here and there. Ken was taking it all in, and by the time Avery finished, an ambulance was pulling into the drive quietly, but with the emergency lights flaring.

"My head is better. I'm not sure a trip to the hospital is necessary." Brynn looked anxiously at the lights flashing outside. The rain had slowed, but it kept coming down steadily as if it had settled in for the night.

"Let the paramedics be the judge of that. You took quite a tumble around the car." Avery looked at the other men, who nodded agreement.

Flint let the man and woman wearing EMS uniforms in the front door and guided them to the victim. After a quick once-over, the medics wrapped her in a shock blanket and began to look at her pupils.

"She doesn't seem to be badly concussed. We can take her to the hospital for a CT scan just to be sure, if you'd like." The female was speaking. "I'll warn you it's a busy night there. Lots of chaos going on in this weather."

"She was knocked unconscious for a pretty good bit. I think it might be best to check her out." Avery gave Brynn a stern look, seeming aware she was about to try to beg off.

She wanted to groan. A trip to the ER didn't sound like fun at all. She just wanted a hot bath and a bed. It seemed they would never get to the safe house.

The paramedics settled her onto a gurney, but Flint McElroy pulled Avery aside before they could get out the door. Brynn wondered vaguely what it was about, but despite her protests, her head still hurt too badly to think too much. She let the female paramedic, who introduced herself as Ashley, hook her up to a blood pressure cuff as they closed the back doors to the ambulance. Ken stood watch, scanning the neighborhood before climbing back into his cruiser. He had offered Avery a ride to the hospital since he wasn't family.

She sincerely hoped Avery made it to the hospital quickly. She was pretty shaken and wasn't sure she had enough wits about her to defend herself if any other problems arose tonight.

Despite the medic's prior warnings, the hospital managed to get her back for CT scans pretty quickly, and Avery met her when they brought her back to the hospital room they had assigned her. "How are you feeling?"

"Not so great. They won't let me go to sleep, even though they gave me something that made me woozy." Brynn smiled a silly smile at him.

"I'm glad they won't. I'm ready to get you out of here." Avery looked around. "I've borrowed a truck from a good friend of mine. He's leaving it in the south lot. The police have been watching the van. They spotted it leaving the scene of the accident and have had a guy on it ever since."

"Why can't they just take them in?" Brynn asked.

"They haven't been able to get them stopped. They keep fleeing." Avery explained. "I'm going to let Ken know when you get released. At least if they still have eyes on them, we should be able to get to the safe house with some protection."

"What if they still follow us?" Brynn was a little disappointed that they couldn't do more.

"The officers will intervene. It's the best we can do right now." Avery seemed to be in agreement, if his expression were to be trusted.

A nurse in purple scrubs came in then, a cup of ice chips in her hand. "The doctor will be in shortly. It looks like they have your CT scan results and you've been moved up to high priority. Someone's looking out for you. This place is terribly busy tonight."

The nurse clicked her tongue as she handed Brynn the ice chips.

"I'm glad to hear it. No offense, but I'd like to get out of here as soon as possible."

Brynn offered her a sweet smile.

"I don't blame you one bit. I'd kind of like out of here tonight, myself. It's going to be a long night." The nurse asked if she needed anything else before turning to go.

As promised, the doctor came in quickly, reading her CT results as he entered. "I'm Dr.

Sean Ingall. It looks like you've only suffered a mild concussion. You'll need to take it easy for a few days, Miss Evans. I'm sending you some scripts as well. Just follow the directions on the labels. I'll have you released in about five minutes." He looked at her and smiled, but it seemed more sympathetic than friendly.

"Thank you, Dr. Ingall. I can leave, then?" Brynn wanted to make sure she had heard correctly.

"Yes, you just have to sign some discharge papers. I'll have security on stand-by to see you out." He nodded at Avery before wishing her well.

"That has to be some kind of record as far as trips to the ER are concerned," she commented to Avery as he helped her into the truck.

"I believe we have Ken to thank for that." Avery smiled broadly.

"How is that?" Brynn didn't understand his amusement.

"His girlfriend is the head nurse in the ER. She told them they'd better get us in and out as quickly as possible or they would all be called on the carpet. Apparently, even the doctors are afraid of her." Avery chuckled.

Brynn giggled, too. "I'm glad I don't work for her, then."

"Me, too." Avery waggled his brows at her before closing the door.

* * *

The safe house was a welcome sight.

It had been the longest of nights and Avery knew Brynn needed rest in a bad way. He could only hope the rest of the night would be more peaceful. The nurses had plied Brynn with warm blankets after getting her into a hospital gown, but she still declared the need for a nice long soak when they got to the house.

Ken Thomas had kindly retrieved their bags from Brynn's car and delivered them to the hospital, though the driver of the wrecker hadn't had to tell anyone the car was totaled. They had little trouble prying the trunk open to get the bags. Avery had changed into dry clothes while waiting on Brynn to get her CT scan.

Once Brynn had gone to clean up, Avery called Camille to let her know they had finally made it. She had asked what was going on, though, so he spent longer than he planned on the phone with her explaining what had happened. She said Martha had tried calling Brynn and couldn't reach her, and she had been worried. Avery assured Camille they were fine, and by the time Brynn emerged from her warm bath, he was almost asleep himself.

Brynn didn't seem to notice as she settled on the cream-colored sofa. "You spoke with Flint a long time before we left. Did he have anything important to say?"

He had hoped they could discuss it after a good night's sleep, but it seemed it wasn't to be. "He thought you were familiar. Said you look just like your mother."

She sucked in a breath. "He knew her?"

Avery nodded. "It was bound to happen. I'm sure there were people in the area who knew her back then."

"Do you think it might've had something to do with why my adoptive parents wanted to move? Even though we lived in Corduroy and my birth parents in Cheyenne, they would have had connections around the area. Maybe I was growing to look more like my birth mother and they didn't think it was safe?" Brynn was making a thoughtful face. He found it adorable, and had to dismiss the warm, protective feelings it brought to the surface.

"That seems like a stretch. Why would it matter? Unless they knew something about your birth parents' deaths." Avery wasn't sure how this all fit together, but it grew more puzzling all the time.

"You're probably right." Brynn put a finger to her lips. "What else did he have to say?"

"Just to be careful." Avery said it absently, but Brynn sat up in response.

"Why did he say that?"

"Just because we had been pursued to his house by armed people trying to kill us, I assumed." He chuckled. It wasn't funny, really, but her response to it had been. "It also goes back to what I mentioned about listening to what people *don't* say."

"Oh. I thought you meant when he recognized me, he said to be careful." Brynn made a sheepish face. "I was still thinking of the rumors Officer Adams mentioned to you. I thought maybe they reached to every corner of the county, and he was referring to those."

It set Avery's mind in motion. Was she right? Had he meant more by the offhand comment? Avery suddenly wondered if Flint McElroy knew more about Brynn's birth parents than he had assumed. He made a mental note to give the man a call in the morning. Maybe he could find out what else Flint knew as well.

"It's funny," Brynn began. "I was so sleepy earlier. Now my mind won't stop racing."

"That's probably good. You shouldn't sleep too much right after a head trauma," Avery reminded her. "What are your thoughts racing about?"

"It was Suzanne Davis again, wasn't it? But, again, she should've been happy that I left town. Still, she followed me. I first thought she only wanted to scare me away from finding out more about my birth parents. But they seem to be growing more desperate to kill me." Brynn shuddered.

Avery considered her words for a moment. "Maybe she's just following orders. Whoever she works for is calling the shots. Someone powerful. It seems that person has ordered her and this man she was with to kill you. Maybe both of us. It sounds like it would be far from the first time these people have killed to keep their secrets."

"What are they trying to hide? What does it have to do with me, and how is it connected to my parents' deaths? We're no closer to figuring this out." She had stood and was pacing in front of the gas fire logs in the living room Avery had lit earlier. The safe house was nicely decorated, he noticed. The whitewashed brick fireplace was accented with slightly rustic farmhouse touches and had a bit of a homey feel to it. It was probably meant to be functional above all things, but it seemed it had been someone's home once.

Avery stopped thinking about the decor and tried to concentrate on Brynn's questions. "My guess would be that they know how, or why, your parents died and don't want you to discover the reason. It's as simple as that."

"But that isn't simple. If they had something to do with it, how have they gotten away with it for all these years?" She seemed upset just thinking about it. He couldn't blame her.

"I suspect if we ever get the cold case files Wilder is working on, we could figure it out. It seems the county isn't very helpful to city police. I hate to get Nick involved with that, but I might have to." Avery stood, too. "There isn't much we can do tonight. I just checked my email again and there's still nothing from Wilder."

She watched him for a second. "Do you think something's wrong?"

Avery started to reply with a negative but thought better of it. It wouldn't be the truth. "I'm not sure. I'm afraid there might be."

She nodded. "Me, too."

Brynn stretched. "Would it be okay if I just lay down? I'm worn out."

"Go ahead. I'll check on you in a little while." He looked away.

Her room was just across the hall from his. He heard the door lock click into place, and hoped she remembered to check the windows as well.

The truth was, he thought a lot of things were wrong. Maybe it was his imagination, but what if someone on the police force in Cheyenne knew something about Brynn's parents' murder? Because that was what it had been. He didn't know why, but someone had silenced Brynn's birth parents, and they thought there was something out there that could lead Brynn to the same evidence.

But how?

It didn't make sense. First, why hadn't her adoptive parents told her she was adopted sooner? Second, why so much secrecy about the identity of her birth parents? Did others suspect the fire hadn't been an accident? If so, why had no one investigated it? And why would Brynn discovering it threaten anyone twenty-seven years later?

He suspected Suzanne Davis knew everything. Somehow, he would get her to talk. For now, he had to try to get some rest.

He checked on Brynn several times in the night. The next morning, he woke to weak, early-morning light and the sound of Brynn clicking keys on her laptop in the sunroom while coffee perked in the kitchen.

"You're getting an early start." He stood in the doorframe, appreciating the way her eyes slanted a little more sharply and her lips curved with a little more fullness from her recent sleep.

She looked up at him with a little gasp. "I didn't mean to wake you. Aunt Martha sent files to me of all the photos she's had preserved and converted to digital from early in my life."

He stepped into the room and sat down beside her on the sofa. "You didn't wake me. I'm usually up before now."

She offered him a small smile. "Good. Coffee is almost ready."

"Great. I'll get the coffee. What have you found so far? Anything helpful?"

"How did you know I was looking for anything specific?" She gave him a sidelong look before going back to the screen.

"Come on, Brynn. I know this is eating you up. What else would have you up at six thirty a.m.? The sun is barely up." Avery tilted his head at her. She seemed to be holding up well, but was that all just what he hoped to see? Maybe on the inside she was falling apart a little.

"I can figure this out. No, I *have* to figure this out." Brynn looked up at him. "The answer is here somewhere."

"You seem to be getting out of sorts about this. I'm here to help. Your emotional state has to be taking a hit here." Avery tried to present his concerns as gently as possible. The last thing he wanted was to upset her further.

She nodded, but emotions played across her features. "You've been very helpful. It's just that looking at this makes me realize how clueless

I was. It seemed like I lived such a normal, ordinary life."

"But that's a good thing, Brynn. A testament to how much your parents loved you." He
thought about his own family's ups and downs.
No one had ever suspected from the outside, but
in their home, it was different.

"I suppose you're right. But it's hard to rec-
oncile the life I had with the life I thought I
had. I guess it'll just take some time to process
it. I'm just not exactly getting time right now."
Her eyes had left the screen again and were focused on his face. He couldn't help wondering
what she was seeing. Her vulnerable expression
made him want to pull her close and share his
strength with her. The attraction seemed to get
stronger with each minute they spent together.

She surprised him by laying a hand on his
forearm. He felt the tingle from her touch all
the way to his insides. "But I'm fine, really. I
will be. I'll be just fine."

He simply nodded at her, still a little stunned
from her gentle touch. "I'll go get coffee."

When he returned, he found her staring at an
old photo of what he assumed was her, her adoptive parents and her aunt. They were wearing
nice clothes and stood in front of what looked
like a church. She was just a few months old
in the picture, if he had to guess. The couple

smiled as the man held her between them and the aunt stood on smiling beside the woman, leaning in as if thrilled for them all.

"Is that your christening?" He handed Brynn a mug as he looked at the photo over her shoulder.

"It looks like it. I've never seen this photo before. Look at that beautiful old church." She outlined the building gently with her fingertip. "I wonder why my parents didn't have a copy of it."

Avery examined all the faces, and then the background. "Can I take a closer look at it?"

Brynn handed over the laptop.

"I know this church." He zoomed in on the photo. "I've seen it before—when I was younger. Maybe the pastor could shed some light on things. He may not still be there, but I would imagine the current pastor could point us in the right direction to find him."

"That could be helpful. And we still haven't reached the fire marshal." Brynn reminded him.

Avery nodded. "Let's see if we can find anything else. It's too early to go around waking pastors and fire marshals. We'll get a plan together and make our phone calls later."

But scrolling through the pictures didn't produce any other clues. Brynn sighed, closing the file. "I wonder if there's anything more."

Avery took her empty mug. "Maybe it's time

to take a break. Get some food. Clear our minds. We can come back to planning our strategy after we eat."

She agreed, but when he went into the kitchen and started rummaging around, she stayed behind for a few moments. He left her to her thoughts while he found some eggs, bread for toast, butter, jelly and milk. He started making scrambled eggs, but when she didn't appear in the kitchen for a few more minutes, he decided to see what she was up to.

He found her on the phone. He stood listening for a moment until he realized she wasn't doing much of the talking. Then he returned to the kitchen and finished preparing the meal.

When she walked into the kitchen a moment later, she wore a stunned look. "Aunt Martha sent me a name for the lawyer who she thought might have my birth parents' will. So I called and spoke to the receptionist at the law firm. She confirmed they had left behind a safe deposit box containing their important documents, but they had requested the box not be opened unless specifically requested by their daughter. She gave me the name of the bank, so I called the bank as well. The woman I spoke to said there is indeed a box that was sealed in the summer of 1994 because the owners were deceased. They signed a provision that their baby girl, should she ever make an inquiry, be allowed to open the box."

He froze. "Do they need proof you are that person?"

"She said the provision says that if I have the key in my possession, that will bear witness to the fact that it is mine to open." Brynn was shaking her head. "I can't believe it."

He stopped spreading jelly over the toast. "Me, either. We'll go as soon as we have eaten. Maybe we'll get some answers."

A little while later they entered the First Bank and Trust and asked for the woman Brynn had spoken with previously.

"Mary Ann Cartwright." She introduced herself at her approach. Her eyes fixed on Brynn for a moment and, if he wasn't mistaken, the woman went a bit pale.

"My name is Brynn Evans. We spoke on the phone." Brynn shook the woman's hand, but to her surprise, before she could even introduce Avery, Ms. Cartwright let her into a private office and closed the door.

"Have a seat for a moment, please." She gestured to the cushioned chairs opposite her desk.

She took up her phone and requested the security officer that was on standby. Once she replaced the phone into the receiver, she clasped her hands together and looked at them. "This is a most unusual circumstance, you understand."

"Of course." Brynn didn't really know what to say. She produced the key. "I expected you would need more proof of my identity."

"Actually… Forgive me for saying so, but all the proof I need is seeing your face, even without the provision. It's like seeing a replica of her." She looked away for a moment then back to Brynn. "I knew your mother well."

Brynn felt her spirits lift instantly. "You did? Can you tell me about her?"

The woman gave her a sad look. "Not here. Maybe we can, um, have coffee one day or something."

Her hopes fell. "I see. No one really wants to talk about my birth parents."

"It was tragic. I suppose no one wants to relive those memories." Ms. Cartwright rose abruptly and stepped to the door. "Well. Let's go see what they've left behind, shall we?"

The security guard met them at the door and Ms. Cartwright opened the locked gateway leading into the safe deposit box room. "It's number twenty-three."

She guided them to a small door and they both inserted their keys. She pulled out a plain, rectangular box and handed it to Brynn. The security guard eyed Avery the entire time.

Brynn looked at him before opening it. She took a deep breath. Avery nodded at her to go ahead.

Inside lay three things. One was a large manila envelope. Probably the will, she assumed. Under it was a large family Bible. The third thing was a locket necklace.

"So these things are mine?" Brynn asked breathlessly.

The woman nodded. "I'd advise leaving the legal documents for now, though, unless you plan to take them straight to your lawyer."

"I wonder why no one read the will. I don't have a lawyer. I've never needed one before now." Brynn was staring at the Bible. Did it hold answers? Her family history? Why her parents were killed? She couldn't care less about the will. She wanted to dig into this Bible.

"Then I'd leave them until you've made an appointment with one. I understood the box was not to be disturbed unless you came for it. There was apparently no one else mentioned in the will. Would you like for me to transfer the fees to your name and reopen the box?" She could feel Ms. Cartwright watching her.

"Yes, please." Brynn placed the envelope back in the box. She held on to the other two items as if her life would go with them.

They closed the box, keyed it back into a locked position, and Ms. Cartwright led them back to her office.

After filling out the necessary paperwork and paying the fees, Brynn felt the woman's eyes on her again.

"Have you been to the house? It's probably in sad shape now." Ms. Cartwright made a tsking sound.

"The Carringtons' house?" Brynn didn't understand. "But I thought their house burned."

She nodded. "Their new house, yes. They built that one after moving out of the one on Cherry Blossom Street. They originally planned to restore it, but later changed their minds."

"It's still there, though? Who owns it now?"

She made a sad face "No one has lived in it for more than a couple of years at a time since. I can only tell you the names of a few families that lived there. The Whites, the Mathisons and the Gable family. But none still live around here. It has been on and off the real estate market. I understand it's for sale now, apparently by some investors."

"Do you know the address?" Brynn asked.

"Sure, but it's the only house for sale on that street. Maybe you could ask the Realtor to show it to you." Ms. Cartwright made a note on the back of a business card and slid it to her. "My personal information is on there as well."

Her expression said she wanted to talk to Brynn, but something was holding her back. Was it fear in her eyes? Did she, too, know more than she could say?

Once they left the bank, Brynn spoke her thoughts to Avery. He agreed.

"Who could be so powerful that they have made everyone in the county afraid?" Avery grasped her hand for a split second.

She pushed down the tender feelings his touch incited in her. "I don't know."

"Contact the Realtor. Let's ask to go have a look. Maybe it will help somehow." Avery seemed to have read her thoughts. She had been about to tell him she intended to do so. She had a nagging feeling in her gut. Something about the house might be a clue about what happened to her parents.

She did as he suggested, and in a few minutes, she disconnected with a smile. "She'll meet us there in thirty minutes."

"Awesome." Avery gave her a grin.

The tiny locket teased her, begging to be explored, so she cracked it open. A lock of hair on either side lay beneath the clasps, one very light blond and the other darker, but somehow very similar.

"This must've been my mother's." She stroked a finger down the darker lock of hair while

Avery looked on helplessly. Tears welled in her eyes for a moment before she closed it and set it aside. She took a deep breath and picked up the Bible then.

Brynn fumbled with it for a second, feeling the weight of Avery's attention on her. When she opened it, a photo stared up at her.

"Avery, look at this. Are those my parents?" She showed him the photo.

"And you as an infant unless I miss my guess. Is that the same church we saw in the other picture? You can only see a little bit of it in the background." He flipped it over. "It has two dates on it, though. 3-14-95 and 12-24-10. How strange."

"Christmas Eve, 2010? My parents died long before that." Brynn shook her head. "Why on earth would that date be on a photo that obviously belonged to my birth parents when I was an infant?"

"I don't know. But I also don't understand why a family Bible would be placed in a lock box with legal documents by a young couple. Unless they knew someone might be coming for them." Avery stared into space a moment, thinking, she assumed.

The thought that her parents expected someone to come after them chilled Brynn, but this new clue thrilled her as well. Were her birth parents entrusting her with finishing something they started?

The idea connected her to them in a way she had never felt before, and it filled her with warmth.

She couldn't let them down.

They had just returned from the bank when Avery finally heard from Wilder. He answered the phone but left the room, leaving Brynn in the living room alone.

"I was getting worried, man. What's going on?" he asked the moment he shut the door to the guest bedroom behind him.

"As soon as I started looking into the cold case files from the Carrington house fire, things started getting weird. It's like I'm being watched." Wilder spoke quietly. "I had to wait until I was off shift to get in touch with you."

"What do you mean, you were being watched?" Avery couldn't understand why anyone would care if he dug into cold case files unless someone there had something to hide.

"I don't know, exactly. I'm sure your suspicions are the same as mine. I hope we aren't dealing with a dirty cop on top of all the other problems with this case, but it looks that way. I found the file, but the folder is missing some things. I can tell because of the creases in the folder. It was much thicker at one time, but now the folder doesn't seem to close in the same place. It's like someone's taken some of the evidence." Wilder was still speaking in low tones.

"Someone took evidence from the file? You're sure?" Avery couldn't believe it. Why would anyone steal evidence from a twenty-something-year-old case file? Unless they were hiding something.

"I'm positive. When I went to the partner of the investigating officer who originally handled the case, he acted strangely. He finally confirmed it. That's when I started to think I was being watched." Wilder paused. "As soon as I left the officer's cubicle, the prickling started. So I acted like I abandoned the whole thing, took the file back to Records, and went back to the other case I'd been working on. But I have been watched ever since."

"You're sure?" Avery asked.

"Cop's instincts, you know?" Wilder said.

"We learned that Brynn's birth parents lived in a house near here before they built the one that burned," Avery told Wilder. "I doubt it'll help, but we plan to go see the house."

Wilder sucked in a breath. "Actually, it might help more than you think."

Avery didn't respond right away. Wilder's reaction didn't make sense. Then he asked, "Why? What do you mean?"

"When I looked at the file, it gave an address—1521 Cherry Blossom Street. But there was mention that the house was searched for evidence related to the reasons for the fire. Nothing was found. But maybe they missed something. Maybe, if someone is trying to cover up a crime, they didn't look as thoroughly as they should've," Wilder said.

"You think the search was botched?"

"Maybe not botched, but maybe they had another reason for going through the house." Wilder sounded thoughtful.

"It's worth a try. We will give the house a good search. I don't know how well it'll work if the real estate agent is too attentive, but maybe she'll give us some space." Avery pondered the scenario.

"Maybe I can take care of that. Send me her name and info and I'll see if I can keep her tied up on the phone while you look around." Wilder paused. "When I get a chance, I'll study up on her listed properties and make sure I can keep her busy for a little while."

"Excellent. I'll text you her info right away." Avery thanked him and disconnected before returning to Brynn.

"I think we might've just gotten a small breakthrough." He smiled when he told her.

As he explained the details, her face lit up. "So maybe my parents left something in the house that will help us figure this whole thing out?"

Avery nodded. "That's exactly what I'm hoping for."

The Realtor was a tiny, middle-aged blonde woman with a contagious smile and bubbly mannerisms. She let them into the house and told them the amenities before letting them look around.

"This is a beautiful house." Brynn made the comment as she admired the cherry stair railing and the paneling in the elegant library that seemed to function also as an office space. It was larger than she had expected, and the craftsmanship was remarkable. It was truly lovely. "Why has no one stayed here and made this their forever home?"

"It's an older home, as you can see, and doesn't quite have all the modernizations many young couples crave. But it would be an easy addition if someone were so inclined. The architecture is amazing." The Realtor gestured around at the huge crown moldings and the sculpted ceilings. Antique light fixtures added historic charm to the spacious rooms and wide doorways with transoms above that provided airflow. The house dated back to a time before air conditioning. But someone had clearly been taking care of it, despite the frequent changes in owners.

"It's gorgeous." Avery was also looking around the lovely old house.

"I'll let you two just look around." The Realtor offered them a brilliant smile. She looked down at her phone as she left.

When she was gone, Brynn turned to Avery. "Where do we start looking?"

She had asked in something of a stage whisper, and Avery turned to be certain the Realtor was gone. In a few seconds, they could see her walk past the window into the yard, cell phone pressed to her ear as she spoke into it with an animated flourish.

"Is there an office? Maybe a file cabinet that was left behind or something like that?" Avery moved across the room, poking his head into doors.

"What about this closet?" Brynn began examining the empty space, which seemed to have been some sort of linen closet at one time. Avery glanced at her through an open door across the hall.

"Any surprises?" He ducked back behind the door to continue his search.

"No. Probably too obvious. There is a weird, deep space behind it, though." She searched it as well. Nothing.

"Old houses like this are bound to have all sorts of secrets." Avery called out the words from another room he was going through.

Brynn leaned around the closet door to see where he was. A quick peek out the window at the end of the hall revealed the Realtor still outside, standing near her SUV now, as she continued to talk on her phone.

"That's true. But we don't have a lot of time to discover the ones we need." Brynn gave up on the closet and went to the stairwell. "I'm going to go look upstairs. There're sure to be more closets. Maybe an attic entry."

The old wood was sturdy, but a couple of the steps in the middle creaked a bit in protest. Brynn found it oddly charming.

She could hear Avery still poking into closets and the kitchen doors below as she searched all the closets upstairs. The attic, also, was full of dust and echoes. After a fruitless search, checking on the Realtor through the windows, she finally decided the attic was too obvious.

Brynn made her way back down the creaking staircase and found Avery standing in the middle of the living room, staring off into his thoughts.

"Nothing?" he asked.

"No. But I think we are looking at the obvious. If you really wanted to keep something hidden, where would you put it? Do you think there could be a secret room or safe somewhere? It is a very old house." Brynn began examining the walls. They seemed solid.

"I think there would be some evidence of it if there was." He moved to some paneling on one of the walls, knocking and listening.

It gave Brynn an idea. "Avery, the stairs. They're solid, but there is one spot that creaks. Maybe it's in the wall beneath those stairs."

Avery walked over to the spot she indicated. He knocked all around it. "It does sound different there, but I don't see how it opens."

"Are you sure?" Brynn examined it also but found nothing. Disappointment filled her. "I guess you're right. I'm all out of ideas." She sat down on the bottom step.

The Realtor poked her head in. "I haven't abandoned you. I'll be right back."

They assured her it was fine, and she went back outside. Avery studied the staircase. After a moment, he began to feel along the outer edges of the steps, where the railing met the wood at the bottom. "About where did the steps begin to creak? Was it the fifth step?"

Brynn turned to look at where he pointed. "Yes, I think so."

"There's an odd groove here." Avery bent to look closer.

This announcement brought Brynn to her feet. "What do you mean?" She crouched just below the step he was looking at.

"Here. It doesn't quite fit the same way as the others." Avery indicated the groove he referred to.

Brynn ran a hand along it. "It isn't completely attached like the others."

It took a little prying, but the top of the step finally moved a little. But only a little.

"It's stuck." Brynn looked to Avery for assistance. "Maybe it's been glued back down or something."

Avery climbed the steps to investigate. With a little force, he finally pried it up.

Below, inside a dusty hollow, sat a small metal box. She carefully opened the lid. Inside was another picture, an envelope and a prayer book. This time the picture was just the church.

"Why would someone leave this here?" She started to reach in for it, but the door swung open below them and the Realtor walked in. She paused when she saw them.

"What are you doing? You're destroying my client's property! I'm calling the police."

TEN

Avery groaned. He hastily covered the crevice below the step.

"We aren't destroying anything. The step was loose," Brynn tried to explain.

The Realtor hurried up the steps to where they stood.

"You're tearing up the staircase?" She looked all around the house as if expecting damage everywhere.

"How would we have pried this up? Do you see any tools? It was a hidden safe box. Old houses often had them built in." Avery stared the woman down.

"Why wouldn't my client have told me?" She was still shaking her head. "It's a good selling point."

"Maybe your client didn't know." Brynn made the suggestion.

"Who owns the house?" Avery asked.

The Realtor frowned. "The house is owned by an investment company."

She didn't say more, and Avery was suddenly suspicious. "What investment company?"

"I really couldn't say. I honestly only work with a lawyer who serves as mediator on the contract." She seemed genuinely unaware, so Avery let it drop. He would look it up later.

The trio looked at one another for a bit longer before the Realtor said, "Unless you plan to make an offer, I need to be going."

Brynn looked at Avery before she answered. She had told the Realtor she was interested in moving back to be closer to her aunt, which was something she had considered after her mother's death. "I think I'm going to need to think about it."

The Realtor nodded. "Okay. Here's my card. If you decide, give me a call."

She gestured toward the door. She was obviously waiting for them to leave so she could lock up.

Avery followed Brynn out. She was moving slowly, obviously reluctant to leave the items behind without looking at them more closely. He couldn't help but wonder what they contained as well, but he didn't see how an old photo and a few papers could hold the answers they sought.

It was strange that there were so many photos of that old church.

They were both silent until they reached the safe house. Once inside and away from listening ears, Avery turned to face her. "I think we can get back in. One of the windows on the south side of the first floor didn't lock properly and I think we can pry it open."

Brynn looked horrified. "Do you mean just break in?"

Avery hesitated. "Well, when you put it like that it sounds pretty bad."

She made a face. "What if we got caught? Is there no other way?"

Avery thought about it for a moment. "I might be able to get Wilder to help us out. But we are going to need a plausible reason that won't raise suspicion. And it will make it much more difficult to keep it quiet. He's having some trouble with the files from the house fire investigation."

"What do you mean?" Brynn looked confused. He hadn't told her about Wilder thinking he was being watched.

"It seems someone in the department wants to keep the case cold. Maybe because they're involved? Or doing a favor for a corrupt friend? Either way, it isn't good. Some of the files are missing and he's being watched. We're going to have to do as much of this as we can on our own."

Brynn put a finger to her lips. "Is it too much of a risk? Do you think it has evidence that Suzanne Davis or her boss is after? From what I could see, it's just a photo. What could possibly be inside that would lead to solving this?"

"I'm not sure. But there might be some reason that they don't want us to find the photo. Or maybe the contents of the envelope. I didn't get a good look. But the good news is that I don't think your attackers know where we are right now." Avery didn't think it would be long before they figured it out, but he didn't really want to bring that up.

She wasn't fooled, however. "Yet, you mean. They'll probably find us soon."

Avery sat down on the edge of the sofa. "That's true. But we have a little time right now. I'm going to try to get in touch with Wilder again. I'll tell him what we've found and see what else he has discovered. Maybe we'll have somewhere to go from there. We need to find out why your parents were targeted. That could lead us to Suzanne's boss."

"Okay. And maybe we can try to reach the fire marshal again." Brynn added the comment. She had a faraway look on her face, and he knew she was probably thinking about not only the fire but the loss of her birth parents once more.

"Are you okay?"

"Yes. I was just thinking about how odd life can be. If my birth parents had lived, I would never have known my adoptive parents. But instead, I was adopted and never knew my birth parents. How am I supposed to know which is for the best?" Brynn's voice cracked a bit. She was likely overwhelmed by everything that had happened in the last few days. The desire to comfort her was stronger than ever.

Avery studied her for a moment. "I can't pretend to know what's best. But I do know that though God's ways are mysterious, he uses our circumstances for good. You can rest assured of that."

Brynn sat very still for a moment before she nodded. "You're right. Thank you."

"Don't thank me." Avery gave her a crooked grin.

Then something changed between them. He couldn't define it, but it was almost tangible. He felt the grin slip from his face, and her expression softened as his must have done the same.

"You have been so good to me, Avery. I can't help but wonder why sometimes." Brynn's expression remained serious.

"I can't seem to help myself." He hadn't meant

to say the words aloud, but now that they floated in the air between them, he couldn't bring them back. He leaned in, hand gently sweeping over the edge of her jawline.

"You could kiss me, you know." She said it so softly he almost thought he dreamed it up, until she gasped softly, presumably at her own boldness.

He didn't wait to see if she changed her mind. He let his lips touch hers softly, and then with a little more courage. She was even softer and sweeter than he had imagined in all those day-dreams he had tried to push from his mind. She was air and light and he needed more of her. He wrapped his arms around her, breathing in her sweet scent.

Reality crashed in with a harsh pang. He pulled away from her. "You shouldn't have let me do that."

A flare of hurt crossed Brynn's face before she could mask it, her limpid eyes shuttering as she turned away.

"No. I suppose I shouldn't have."

But she didn't say any more.

Brynn wanted to run.

The heat of embarrassment drew her palms to her cheeks as soon as he was gone from the room. He walked down the hall without saying anything else and she was happy to just let him go this time. She needed a moment to absorb what had just transpired.

She had asked Avery Thorpe to kiss her.

In all her life, she couldn't think of a more mortifying thing she had ever done.

Or a more exhilarating one.

She touched her lips and fought the urge to giggle. *She had asked Avery Thorpe to kiss her. And he had done it.*

She was acting silly, but even though neither of them wanted a relationship, she couldn't say she was sorry he had kissed her. Then again, maybe she was, because now that she knew how tender his kiss was, she would only want to kiss him again.

She felt ridiculous. And elated.

But how did he feel?

She told herself it didn't matter because it wouldn't happen again. A relationship wasn't going anywhere between them. Friends. Just friends. And friends didn't go around kissing each other.

The reminder that they were both happily single sobered her thoughts a little, and she forced herself to concentrate on what they needed to do next. Part of her still wanted to tell her aunt what she had learned, but the danger was far from over.

She worried it had just begun. And just like that, she was thinking about the fire again. It haunted her that her father had died after saving her. She wondered what might have happened if he had saved her mother first. Or if they would have survived… How different would her life have been? Would she have ever known her adoptive parents?

It scared her to think of how differently things could have turned out for them all, yet it saddened her that she had never actually known her mom and dad. It was the most confusing feeling she had ever experienced in her life. Well, nearly, anyway. The most confusing had to be her feelings for Avery Thorpe.

He came back into the room after a little while, freshly showered and looking like any woman's dream guy. Brynn started to speak, but he beat her to it.

"I have to say something, Brynn. I'm sorry for what I said, and I'm sorry for kissing you. I certainly didn't mean to lead you on or play with your feelings in any way. I enjoyed it, maybe a little too much, actually. But we both know where we stand on relationships. So…well, I'm sorry." His contrite expression only endeared him to her more, and she had to swallow back a lump in her throat. He was a good man and she wished with all of her being that he could be hers. But she knew it couldn't happen. Her trust would only extend so far, and a relationship was out of the question.

"Thank you, Avery, and…well, I'm sorry too." She paused only a moment, debating. But he deserved to know. "It isn't easy for me to trust anyone after what happened with my last boyfriend."

He tilted his head. "I can definitely relate to that."

She offered him a small smile. "We just need some space. Maybe once this is all over and we spend some time apart, we can see things more clearly."

He made a sound of agreement, but it sent a pang of regret through her. She knew it was the right thing, but the idea of spending time away from Avery made her heart sick.

The moment hadn't passed before they were interrupted by Brynn's cheerful ringtone.

"I don't know this number. Who could it be?" She stared at the screen. The phone didn't refer to it as possible spam, so she was curious over whether she should answer it.

Before she could decide, Avery asked for the phone.

"Avery Thorpe." He listened a moment before a skeptical expression crossed his handsome features. He hummed out a couple of noncommittal responses.

"Okay. We will meet you there in about forty-five minutes." Avery disconnected the phone and returned it to her.

"Wilder has a warrant for us. He wants us to meet him at the Cargill House." Avery led her out the door.

They didn't speak on the way, both still avoiding the topic of what had transpired between them. However, long before they pulled into town, they saw smoke billowing high into the sky. The possibilities were obvious. Yet neither of them spoke as they neared their destination. Brynn felt her insides churning.

Someone was sending a message—a message that they knew every move Brynn and Avery made.

And they weren't about to give up their secrets that easily.

She heard Avery speaking into the phone to Wilder as they pulled to a stop just down the street a ways from Cargill House, and a chill shuddered through her. Fire trucks and emergency vehicles were now beginning to line the road.

"No need to bother with that warrant, Wilder," Avery said. "Cargill House is completely engulfed in flames."

ELEVEN

The lights from the fire trucks sitting along the curb in front of Cargill House cast moving shadows against the house and all the surrounding buildings with their red glow as Avery sprinted up to see if he could be of any help.

"Not much we can do, other than put out the fire at this point. Place is completely destroyed." A stony-faced fireman just shook his head as he offered the reply. "Appreciate that, though, Mr. Thorpe."

He investigated the guy's soot-blackened face where reverse raccoon eyes were staring back at him. "Sorry, Beckett. Didn't recognize you at first. No one was inside?"

"Nope. We cleared it before the smoke got too intense. These old houses burn hot and fast." Beckett clucked his tongue and ducked back over to his squadron, who battled the flames.

And anything left inside was sure to have long since gone up in smoke.

This guy had some MO. Kill. Burn. Destroy. Anything to keep his secrets hidden. But he seemed to keep getting away with it. And Avery couldn't help feeling like burning the house was another message. *Yes, you are close. Yes, I'm still watching you. No, you can't win this because I'm a step ahead of you.*

The thing Avery hated most about that message was that as of this moment, its sender was correct. He was winning.

He glanced back to see where Brynn had gone, just in time to catch a glimpse of movement several yards away. The glint of the lights from the fire trucks hit the short barrel of a pistol.

"Brynn, get down!" He dove for her, but she was already hitting the ground.

He belly-crawled toward her and rolled with her toward the shelter of the fire trucks. Once she was securely ensconced behind one, Avery pulled his Glock and ran toward the spot where he had seen the figure. He stayed low, and another shot plastered the concrete near his feet. He kept moving, trying to get to the gunman before he could hit him.

The shadowy figure darted away, but then the lights flashed off the gun again. Avery ducked before dropping to the ground and rolling toward the figure, his shoulder wound burning anew at the impact.

Ignoring it as best he could, he jumped back to his feet and chased the gunman after the bullet just missed him. He was running across the yard toward the neighboring house, his feet flying over the ground. He was almost close enough to make out the figure now, crouching behind a neighboring shed, when the gunman lowered the pistol to his side and took off at a sprint.

Avery was quick, though, and he had no trouble gaining on him. He dove for the gunman, but the other man was thick and strong and managed to wrest away from Avery's grip.

"Stop!" Avery called, running after him. "I don't want to shoot but I will."

The man didn't respond.

Avery fired a warning shot over his head, but the dark-clad figure kept running.

He paused and took aim again, this time not planning to miss. He pointed his Glock at the man's thigh.

With a grunt, the gunman flopped to the ground, howling in pain. He tried to stand again, but fell back into the grass of the yard, whimpering like an injured animal.

Avery rushed toward him, but the man wasn't out of fight yet. He raised his pistol with a shaking hand and aimed it at Avery once more. "You stop. I won't hit you in the leg. I shoot to kill."

Avery stopped and threw up his hands. The man grinned menacingly beneath his toboggan hat. Avery couldn't be sure in the darkness, but he thought he had seen the man before.

"Tell your lady friend we are coming for her. And we won't stop until she's dead." The man cackled and strained to his feet. He started backing slowly away at a limp. Avery could only watch helplessly as he held the gun on him until he struggled into an old jalopy sitting down the street along the curb.

When the man slammed the door and peeled away from the curb, Avery rushed for his gun and tried to shoot out the tires, but he was too far away for the Glock's short range. He looked for a tag, but the old car didn't have one. He probably couldn't have made out what it said in the dark anyway.

He made his way back to Brynn as he called in the description of the car. As he did so, he wondered if any of the local police were even following up on Brynn's case. If his suspicions were correct, they probably weren't.

Whoever had Brynn on their radar seemed to have the whole town in his pocket.

Luke Miller was no exception.

He wouldn't agree to meet at a public place, nor would the former fire marshal allow Avery to come to his home, immediately arousing Avery's suspicion in the man's innocence. Miller had insisted he just wanted to keep things quiet and didn't want to look like a snitch by talking to a private investigator.

In either case, Avery didn't trust the man.

When Avery and Brynn arrived at the old, abandoned home place that Miller had suggested they use as a meeting place, the man was pacing just beyond the redbrick chimney that marked the last remaining bit of the house still intact. It was out in the hills in a secluded location overgrown with vegetation. The area was owned by the county and no one visited the place unless they were just out four-wheeling or exploring. Miller stopped and looked up when he heard the tires on the old dirt road. Lines on his face and a haggard expression made Avery think the man had seen too much in his lifetime. It had begun to catch up with him.

Avery greeted him with a nod as he stepped from the vehicle, but Miller was focused on Brynn. "What's she doing here? I thought you just wanted to ask me some questions about an old fire investigation."

"This concerns her as well." Avery frowned at the man before looking back at Brynn. Why was he so concerned about Brynn's presence?

Miller didn't respond, but simply stared at Brynn. Avery got the feeling the man was seeing a ghost, so to speak. Had he known Brynn's mother also? It had become obvious that everyone who had known Rebecca Carrington thought Brynn was the very image of her birth mother.

"The fire occurred back in the spring of 1994, and it involved the death of Anderson and Rebecca Carrington." Avery began.

"I know what fire you're asking about. What I don't know is why you want to question me. I have nothing to say. It's all in the files." His tone was sharp and unfriendly. He clearly didn't want to talk.

This might prove more difficult than Avery had first thought. He didn't like the feeling he got when he looked Luke Miller in the eye.

"Some information is missing. I believe you might be able to help us." Avery spoke in a composed, unruffled tone. He had found the best way to get people to open up wasn't to meet them at their level, but to appeal to them calmly and carefully.

Miller didn't reply immediately, still eyeing Brynn with what he could only assume was discomfort. "Anything you want to know was broadcast everywhere. It was all over the news and the papers."

"Mr. Miller, I understand that I was found under a tree in the yard when the firemen arrived on the scene?" Brynn took the interrogation into her own hands. "Do you remember any details about who found me or who else was around at the time?"

The man grunted. "I don't know why it matters, but a fireman named Trenton Holmes found you. He moved out of state a couple of years ago, though, so I doubt you can find him easily, if that's what you're thinking."

"Trenton Holmes. Hmm. Okay. And he brought me to you?" Brynn typed the name into the notes on her phone.

He cleared his throat. "No. I wasn't there at the time. As I understand it, he took the baby to the paramedics on the scene and that was the end of it."

Brynn leaned toward him. "You arrived later? After firefighters had put out the fire? You don't know what the paramedics did after taking me in?"

"I got there while the men were still battling the fire. But the baby was gone by then."

Miller's eyes shifted from Brynn to the old brick chimney and back again. He was trying to avoid something. Avery remarked, "Most of the details were reported in the news, as you said, but one very important detail was not. What we never found was the cause of the fire. It was reported as unknown."

"It *was* unknown. No sign of foul play." Miller snapped out the words. "You think you're the first to have suspicions?"

Brynn's face reddened. "And how were those suspicions laid to rest? All I am asking for is some reassurance that my parents' deaths were an accident—that everything was done that could be done to be sure they weren't murdered."

Miller's eyes narrowed. "I don't like what you're implying. All I can tell you is that my investigation found no signs of arson."

When he refused to continue, Avery decided to press him for more information. "What did you find? You and I both know a lot of fires are started without obvious signs of arson. Were you sure? We know that Brynn was found outside under a tree as soon as firefighters arrived on the scene. The house was already up in flames, reported by a neighbor. Reports also had her father inside the house with her mother. I'm sure autopsies were completed. What did it say in the reports?"

"Are you suggesting we didn't do a thorough investigation?" Miller's face had become mottled, and his voice had risen an octave.

Avery's voice was dead calm. "Did you? Or did you simply write it off as what it was staged to look like? An accidental house fire where two people died of smoke inhalation before they could get out of the burning structure."

"Staged? You think the whole thing was a setup? And what do you know about fire, Mr. Thorpe? Just because you're a detective, you think you know everything there is to know about investigating? That's not in your wheelhouse." Miller stepped toward him.

"I know enough. I know something had to start it. I know that if a person knows enough about fire, they can make it look like an accident. I know that any fire investigator worth his salt can find the cause, even if it was started by accident. A candle left burning too close to the upholstery, an ember that escaped a fireplace unseen to ignite a rug or the carpet, faulty wiring, grease left cooking too long on the stove... But in the middle of the night when no one was stirring? It was a new construction home. Wiring would have had to pass inspection. There was a new baby in the house. It seems unlikely such a couple would be so careless."

Miller's brow had sunk low over his eyes, his forehead now his most prominent feature. Anger stilted his response. "It depends on the couple."

Brynn cocked her head sideways at him before stepping close. "Why couldn't you find the cause, Mr. Miller?"

He stared at them both for a long moment.

Then he unexpectedly shoved his hands into his front pockets and slumped forward. "I had to stop investigating."

The words were so quiet Avery wondered if he had heard correctly. "What? Why would you have to stop?"

Miller's whole demeanor had changed. "I was ordered to do so. It would have cost me my job had I refused. I couldn't afford to let that happen."

"But who could order you to stop the investigation? How can anyone do that?" Brynn was incredulous.

"I can't say. I won't put my life in danger now for something that happened almost thirty years ago." Miller shook his head. "And if you so much as breathe a word that I said so, I'll find you and make you regret it. I have to be going."

"What if we can get you protection? Would you be willing to testify if we could ensure your safety?" Avery wasn't giving up so easily. If Brynn's parents were murdered and it was covered up, this man knew who did the covering up.

"There's no way you could possibly protect me from him."

Avery read stark fear on the man's face just before he turned and strode away.

"Who could he possibly be so afraid of? After all this time?" Brynn clasped a knuckle between her teeth as she paced back and forth across the safe house living room. "Why wouldn't he want to put the man behind bars if he murdered my parents?"

Avery watched her with a contrite expression. "It's not always that simple, Brynn. The man has a family. He didn't finish the investigation, so he doesn't know for sure it was murder."

"How could he not at least be suspicious in such a situation?" Brynn shook her head. "He had to have known."

"We will put together a list of people who could have had such sway in Miller's life at the time. But it will take a little bit of time. City records should have the names of people he worked for and with. Finding dates and times might be the tedious part." Avery was writing something in a notebook. His phone chimed and he looked at it.

"What is it?" Brynn could see the tiny bit of hope flare in his eyes as he read.

"Wilder has managed to get a warrant to search your parents' old house. We are going back there and checking out the hidden stair panel again." He shot her a grin.

"When?" She stopped pacing at last, only just realizing she had been wearing a hole in the floor.

"He's on his way with it now. Less than fifteen minutes." Avery grinned.

When Wilder arrived, Avery made the introductions, and they wasted no time heading over to the house to explore it further.

"Thank you for doing this, Wilder." Brynn smiled at him. "It means a lot to me."

"I hope it helps. I'm sorry about the files. I kept hoping the missing pages would turn up somehow, but it seems someone has made them disappear." Wilder looked at Avery. "There are a lot of missing pieces to this case."

"We are trying to eliminate that problem." Avery told him what they had learned from Luke Miller.

Wilder whistled low. "I wonder what he really knows. It must be big."

"We already know there might be corruption somewhere in local law enforcement, but who would be powerful enough to stop an arson investigation?" Avery was talking as they walked, keeping an eye out for anyone who might overhear.

"I'm afraid of the answer to that. It seems to be more than just a bad cop in this case." Wilder lowered his voice even more. "And whoever's covering it up seems to still have plenty of power over the locals. Even those who have retired."

He was referring to Miller. It did seem odd that the former fire marshal had dropped the investigation for fear of losing his job at the time, but now he seemed to be afraid for his very life. Brynn shivered at the thought. The perpetrator had committed murder before. Of course, he would continue to kill to keep things quiet.

Like he had tried to do to her.

When they had called the real estate agency, they agreed to send someone out with a key. It wasn't the same Realtor whom they'd met before, and the young lady let them in and stayed outside.

The house was much as they had left it. Wilder remarked on how interesting he found the old architecture and Brynn decided she liked Avery's friend. When she led them back to the stairs and they opened the secret hiding place below the step, Wilder sucked in a breath.

"Wow. Just like the old Hardy Boys or Scooby Doo mysteries." He breathed the words with a little laugh.

He grinned. "My grandma. She loved mysteries. I read a couple of her old Nancy Drew books also. She shared all the vintage mystery stuff with me."

Brynn's laugh tinkled through the house. "I must admit I've read my share of Nancy Drew books as well. I read some newer ones as a young girl, but then the librarian at school introduced me to some of the originals from way back."

Avery was shaking his head at them both. "Wow. Vintage mystery buffs. What's next? Agatha Christie? Sherlock Holmes?"

When the pair of them gave a telling laugh, Avery just pulled out the box. "I feel like I've missed out on something."

"You have. Classics." Wilder elbowed him. "You should catch up."

But the banter ceased when they looked into the box. Under the papers they had earlier seen, there was a prayer book and a tiny bracelet. "That bracelet. It's so beautiful." Brynn reached for it.

"Careful." Avery cautioned. But she fingered it delicately, gently releasing the clasp on the tiny locket. Two locks of hair entwined sat in the opening. One white blond, the other a little darker, but obviously from mother and tiny child.

"Just like in the necklace." She turned it over and saw a name engraved there.

Avery whistled low. "It matches the necklace you found in the safe deposit box."

"Brittania Rebecca Carrington." Brynn read the name aloud. "Was this my mother's?"

Avery took the bracelet from her hand. "No, it's too small. Look. The chain would never reach around an adult wrist. This was yours."

Wilder watched in silence. Brynn felt his empathy, though, as if it were a palpable thing.

"My name must have been changed after the adoption. Not just my last name, but my first and middle as well. My legal name is Brynn Elizabeth Evans now. I wonder if it was because my adoptive parents knew someone could link me to my birth parents if it wasn't changed." Brynn was speaking her thoughts aloud.

"It's a small town, Brynn. People would have known you were adopted anyway." Avery looked to Wilder, who was shaking his head.

"Yes, but maybe they wouldn't have known who her birth parents were as she grew older if her name was changed," Wilder added. "No one could have known for sure that she was the child found at the fire that night."

Brynn stroked the hair in the locket as Avery pulled the prayer book from the dusty box.

"Until she started to look just like her mother." Avery held up the old photo that had fallen out of the box. Brynn's parents smiled back at them, her mother an almost exact replica of Brynn. "You might have been right about that theory, Brynn."

"That's almost creepy." Wilder stared at the photo. Rebecca Carrington, around the same age as Brynn at the time, stared back at them in a bridal gown.

"So my adoptive parents moved away. Do you think someone was threatening them, too? I don't understand why my mere existence would be a threat to someone who had committed murder so long ago and gotten away with it." Brynn held out her hands for the photo.

"Unless they knew you would eventually start asking questions. Someone was bound to mention that you looked like Rebecca Carrington. If you learned you were adopted, heard about the fire, it would naturally all begin to come together for you. Maybe, like you said, your adoptive parents moved you away to keep that from happening." Avery watched her carefully.

"I really just want to get this all back to the safe house and see if we can make any sense of it all." Brynn's voice trailed off and she sucked in a breath. "Avery, is this the same church in the other photo?"

He took it and studied the building. "It is. I wonder what the connection is. The other photo was just the church."

He picked up the one they had seen when they initially found the box, cast aside as they looked at the other contents. The back of it simply read, "Store up your treasures."

"That's from the Bible. It's from Matthew 6:20, but it's not the whole verse. What is that about? Just a reminder? Or a clue?" Brynn placed a finger against her lips.

"There has to be a reason the church is in so

many of the pictures your mother hid." Avery
pointed out.

Wilder looked at it and shrugged. "Maybe
it was a popular place of worship at the time."

Avery flipped the other photo over. "A Bible
verse."

Brynn studied it. "Psalm 91 verse 15. *He shall
call upon me and I will answer him. I will be
with him in trouble. I will deliver him and honour him.* That's a favorite verse of mine."

She opened the prayer book and found it was
full of writing in her mother's hand. "Look at
this. My mother must have kept notes on all the
sermons she heard." She flipped through the
pages and began to skim through the words. "I
can't wait to read these."

At the top of one page, a verse stood out, written in large, capital letters. Brynn studied it.
"This one seems to have made quite an impact."

Wilder had come closer to look at it as well.
"Proverbs 21:21. Do you remember that one?"

"No, I can't say I do." Brynn scanned down
the page. Her finger stopped, pointing. "Here
it is."

Avery read the verse from the page. "*He that
followeth after righteousness and mercy findeth life, righteousness, and honour.* And it's
dated the same as that photo from your christening. 3/14/95. But look. The other date is writ-

ten under it. 12/24/10. Too far in the future for them to know what it holds."

"Dedicated to their firstborn child?" Wilder asked. "But maybe the other isn't a date at all."

Brynn's brow furrowed. "Maybe. But what is it?"

"Maybe a message of another sort." Avery shrugged.

"I think we should find where this church is and pay it a visit." Brynn didn't mind expressing her opinion about it. Wilder grinned at Avery over Brynn's head. He must be thinking along the same lines.

"First, should we go back to get the Bible and locket necklace from the safe house?" Avery tried not to grin back at his friend.

The door came open and the first real estate agent that they had spoken to came in, still giving the younger woman an earful. "This home belongs to *my* client. You should have waited for me."

Then she turned on them. "What do you think you are doing? Isn't it enough that you destroyed that staircase before? You came back to take something that doesn't belong to you?"

"Actually, I think it does." Wilder said this quietly.

"My client will sue. You don't want to get crossways with him. Unless you plan to buy the house, you have no business here." The real estate agent was red in the face now.

"We have a warrant." Avery brushed past her.

"Why? What's going on?" She began to back up. The younger woman stood behind her, trying not to smile. She was clearly happy to see the woman on the receiving end of the demands.

Wilder stepped toward her and flipped open his badge. "I'm Detective Wilder Hawthorne with the Cheyenne Police Department. We're conducting an investigation. That's all you need to know."

The woman started stammering and put her hands in front of her in a gesture of surrender. "I'm only trying to sell the house. It's owned by the Parham Holdings Company." She didn't say anymore, but she didn't have to.

"Yes, we know. The Parham Holdings Company that owns the Shadow Acres nursing homes? The one owned by the brother of District Attorney Clifford Parham?" Avery stared at her. "Why do they own this house?"

"It isn't unusual for companies to invest in real estate and then later sell it. Maybe they had intentions of using it for their business and changed their minds." The real estate agent was still trying to back up. She had her cell phone in her hand.

Avery didn't look convinced. "I'd like to talk to Mr. Parham about that personally."

"Like I said, I only work with a mediator." She inched toward the door a little more. Brynn set down the prayer book and photo and moved down to block her path. She wanted some answers, and it seemed this woman had some of them.

"We need your contact information for the mediator, then." Wilder closed in from one side while Avery stepped closer on the other. With Brynn behind her, she couldn't go anywhere.

"This is borderline harassment. I am not obligated to give out that information." She looked worse than frazzled.

"We are looking into a cold case. It's possible that the previous owners of this house were murdered. That would be an excellent selling point for you, I'm sure." Avery fixed her with a raised eyebrow.

"What? How do you know that?" She looked panic-stricken.

"You answer our questions first." Wilder tilted his head at her but didn't smile.

"I can't." She whispered the words. "They're watching."

TWELVE

"Who?" Avery demanded. "Who's watching?"

"Shhh!" the woman begged. "I don't know who they are. But they know everything."

Avery was about to give up and decide the woman was just having a breakdown of some sort, when she pulled out a card. She scribbled something on it and handed it to him. In a louder voice, she said, "Give me a call when you want to discuss the particulars."

He read the name on her card, Samantha Barnes, and frowned at her. She raised her brows and he turned it over. On the back was written an address. It seemed familiar somehow, but he couldn't quite place it.

"Thank you, Ms. Barnes. We will." Avery decided to play along. Whatever she was up to, it was strange.

"You can take the box if you like." She said this quietly before striding out the door. "Amanda will lock up when you're done."

While Amanda waited, they secured the top of the step back in place and left the house. The young woman nodded and thanked them with a nervous smile.

When she was out of sight, they made their way silently to Wilder's truck. Avery spoke quietly to Brynn. "Get in. We need to go for a drive."

He helped Brynn into the truck first, then climbed in beside her. He waited until the doors were closed. "There's an address she wrote on the back of this card," he said.

"Why? What could it be for?" Wilder settled behind the wheel and pushed the ignition start button.

"I don't know. But maybe we should put the address into the GPS and find out. She didn't put a time down, or I would have assumed she wanted to meet us there, to talk somewhere away from whoever she thinks is watching."

"That would have made more sense." Wilder waited while he entered the address. It popped up on the screen and the three of them stared at it.

"A church?" Wilder asked.

Brynn and Avery looked at one another. He had thought the address sounded familiar. "*The* church? The one from the photos?"

"What all do you guys know about this church?"

Wilder looked really confused as he put the truck in gear.

"There was another photo of my birth parents and me at my christening. One I had never seen before. It had some dates written on the back. More than one. I could understand dating it for when it was taken, but the other date didn't make sense. It was when I was much older. It said 12-24-10. That was fifteen years after my parents died." Brynn explained as best she could.

"Maybe it wasn't a date?" Wilder suggested.

"What else could it be?" Brynn's forehead wrinkled.

"I don't know, but maybe the church will have some answers," Avery commented.

They arrived at the church about fifteen minutes later to see it was empty and abandoned. It didn't look like it had held services for at least twenty years. The windows were boarded up and the parking lot was grown up with weeds.

"It's decrepit. What could she have sent us here for?" Wilder was shaking his head.

Avery opened the door. "She knows something. Maybe she plans to meet us here somehow."

"Are you going inside?" Brynn asked. "It looks like it could fall down around us."

"I think it's safe enough." Avery stepped

over some litter strewn along the sidewalk and pushed on the door. It was locked. "Wilder, I'm going to need your skills over here."

His buddy grinned, knowing right away the skills to which Avery referred. "I haven't gotten the chance to pick a lock in a little while. This should be fun."

"Is this legal?" Brynn was asking. "I mean, it's clearly abandoned, but surely someone still owns it."

Avery did a quick search on his phone while Wilder worked at the lock. "The congregation. It seems that the attendees bought the building and property from the denomination it was formerly owned under, shortly before it ceased to hold services. So it is basically owned by the public. No one in particular."

"And then who holds the keys? Why is it locked if no one in particular owns it?" Brynn's brow wrinkled.

"Probably the city. It likely had to be locked to prevent vagrants and kids from taking shelter there and causing damage to the property." Avery shrugged. "It's a bigger problem than you would think."

"Got it." Wilder's tone held a note of triumph. He swung the door open. "Let's go."

Avery led the way, leaving Brynn between himself and Wilder. They had barely gotten inside, however, when shots began to ping on the side of the old rock church building. Wilder gave Brynn a little push and Avery grabbed her and pulled her down as Wilder closed the heavy door and locked it. A stained glass window shattered somewhere above their heads.

"A trap?" Brynn asked.

"Maybe. Or maybe she was telling the truth about being watched. Hard to tell." Avery crawled along the dust-coated floor. "Stay down."

The shots continued to pepper the rock walls, until they heard running feet. Someone worked at the door latch, rattling the old iron handle. It didn't give, and the feet ran around the building again. More windows shattered. Avery ushered Brynn under an ancient wooden pew.

Avery felt in his pocket, but his phone wasn't there. He must have left it in the truck. "Brynn, call 911. I don't have my phone."

She nodded and reached for it. "Uh-oh."

"What's wrong?" Avery didn't like her tone.

"No service. How can that be?" She moved the phone around, sticking it out from under the pew to look for a signal. She yanked it back when more glass shattered, raining around the room. Shots came from the other end of the building then.

Wilder was under a pew just in front of them.

He was checking his phone as well. "Me, neither. There must be a tower out or something. Great timing."

Avery groaned. "We're surrounded."

Wilder nodded. "I'll cover the back. You stay with Brynn."

Avery pulled his gun. "Got it. Do you have your backup piece on you?"

Wilder paused. "Of course. Do you need it?"

He inclined his head toward Brynn. Wilder's eyes widened. "She can shoot?"

"She can now," Avery said as Wilder took out his extra 9mm and handed it to Brynn. She looked at it for a second, then glanced back at Wilder. She took the gun carefully in hand.

"Just make sure you don't hesitate. If you miss, it might not end well."

Brynn's stomach rolled over, and a cold sweat gathered on her palms and forehead.

It had been one thing to point a gun at a paper target. Thinking about taking a human life did something else altogether inside of her. Could she do it if it came down to hers or someone else's? She hoped so.

Lord, give me wisdom. I don't like the kind of power this weapon gives me, she prayed silently, knowing Avery still watched her. Wilder had gone through the sanctuary and down the narrow hall that had once held Sunday school classrooms.

More shots came, prodding her into action. She gave Avery a single nod, and he pointed to a low window. "I'll be right here across from you. If you see anyone, don't hesitate."

Her face must have been pale. He didn't move right away. Instead, he squeezed her free hand. "You can do this, Brynn. It's necessary. Life or death. This has to end before they take your life."

She knew he was right. And her birth parents were counting on her. She positioned herself at the window, just out of sight. Her hands cupped the pistol, and she took a deep breath. She could hear Wilder firing from the back of the building. Shots answered. A side door rattled. How many people were out there?

It was a tiny church. The stained glass windows lay shattered and glinting from the floor. Everything seemed to slow down as she looked around at the destruction. The smell of dust and disuse clustered in her nostrils. It was a fortress, though. The windows might be shattering, but the rock walls were virtually indestructible.

She felt a comforting presence as she remembered this was a house of God. She would be protected here. Her grip strengthened on the

9mm as Avery took fire. She raised herself just enough to see out the window.

There was no one there at first. But a second later a shadow flitted across the cracked sidewalk just in front of her. She took aim and waited, cupping the pistol as Avery had taught her. *Don't hesitate. Don't hesitate.*

The figure appeared, gun at the ready, and she fired. The figure fell.

She almost passed out herself as she slumped back down below the window.

"Avery!" She called his name breathlessly. "Avery, I hit someone."

Avery almost dropped his own weapon. He had thought his words to Brynn would empower her. Just allow her enough courage to protect herself. But maybe his words about her saving her own life had been more effective than he had expected.

She had definitely gone on the offensive.

"Stay calm. We aren't out of this yet." He glanced out the window on his side.

"How many do you think there are?" Brynn's voice sounded high and anxious now.

"I don't know, but it isn't over yet. Just breathe. It will be okay. Surely someone will have reported the shooting by now. Police should be here before long." He took up position again after noticing Brynn do the same. She was a strong woman. Her shoulders squared and he knew she was setting her mind on business.

A shot came through a window in the hall and a crash sounded. He looked at Brynn, whose eyes had gone wide. "Should we check on Wilder?"

He nodded. He was more concerned someone had shot it out to crawl inside. "Stay behind me."

They eased the door from the sanctuary open and crept into the hall. No one had climbed in, so they moved closer to investigate. A chunk of plaster had fallen, revealing an odd set of lines in the wall. A large, framed print of a Bible verse lay amid the rubble.

"Is that a hidden panel? A wall safe or something?" Brynn felt along the lines that had been covered by the print. It gave a little and the lines gave way, opening to reveal a locked cabinet safe.

Avery stepped closer to investigate. "I think you're right."

She stooped to examine the print, brushing off some dirt and debris with one hand. "Look at this. It's the same verse that we found in the prayer book. Proverbs 21:21. *He that followeth after righteousness and mercy findeth life, righteousness, and honour.* What does it mean?"

Avery tried the door of the old cabinet. It was locked, of course. An old-fashioned combination lock jutted out slightly on one end.

"Whatever it is, it doesn't look like anyone has opened it in a long time."

Brynn stared at the safe in amazement. Her gut told her this was important. "How will you get it open?"

Avery was about to reply when a flare of lightning streaked the room in harsh light before it fell back into shadows again. He waited for the loud crack of thunder to subside. "I think I might know what those odd dates were. Not dates at all."

Brynn made a sound of understanding.

The sky opened up at that moment, leaving them little doubt that their attackers outside had indeed taken shelter elsewhere for the moment.

Wilder called out a second or two later. "I think we have lost them for the moment. I'm going to try to make a break for the truck and call 911."

Avery acknowledged his words. Brynn gave him an odd look.

"You aren't going to tell him what we found?" she asked.

"It may be nothing. And besides, he will be back soon, I'm sure." Avery shrugged.

"Or we will be out. Whatever's in that safe can go with us, right?" Brynn tried to hide her shiver at the thought of staying in the creepy old space much longer in the dark. Storm clouds had obliterated any remaining light in the old stone building.

Avery pressed his lips together. "It depends on what it is. Your mother seemed to be leaving you clues about something, but we have no idea what. Whatever it is could have gotten her killed."

Brynn did as Avery asked, shining the light steadily on the combination lock jutting out from the safe. The numbers were worn. "Can you see the numbers to try the lock? It's so old."

Avery leaned closer to the wall. "I think so."

Brynn stood silently as Avery tried the safe. On the last number, he turned the dial and she waited, holding her breath.

Nothing happened.

Avery sighed. "Maybe that wasn't it."

Brynn blew out a deep breath. "It has to be. Try it again. Please."

He did, and this time the lock caught, sticking on a wrong number and wouldn't budge. "It's not going to work. It's so old and it probably hasn't been opened in a long time. It's sticking, probably from rust and disuse."

Brynn squeaked out a sound of disappoint-ment. "Can we try some WD-40 or something?"

Avery gave her an exasperated look. "Did you happen to bring any?"

She tried to laugh, but it came out weak and ineffective. "Not today.'

Avery let out a breath. "You know, I have some in my truck. Too bad it's in the shop."

"Of course you do." She smiled. "That's such a guy thing. You'll be a great dad one day."

She had meant it to tease him, but the idea made her breath catch in her chest. He would be a great dad, for sure. But she shouldn't be imagining him as a father to a child of her own. She had long since decided she wouldn't be a mother. Not with the way she handled relation-ships.

He looked at her, too, his intense expression not helping her derail her thoughts at all. He seemed to be thinking along the same lines she was, if the look he wore was any indication. He was shaking his head.

"I'll stick to being an uncle." He turned back to the safe. "Let me try one more time."

"Are you an uncle?" Brynn asked the ques-tion as he turned away, glad to have something else to occupy her thoughts.

"Actually, yes. My brother Grayson adopted a little girl recently. And I just got news that

Briggs and Madison are going to have a baby soon also. Too bad none of them will move back to Wyoming and let me spoil my nieces and nephews." He worked at the lock again, jiggling the dial loose.

"I'm sure you would do an excellent job of that." Brynn smiled at the thought.

He fell silent as he worked at twisting the lock dial carefully once again. She wasn't holding her breath this time, though, so when there was a *thunk* and the door creaked open a fraction, she was shocked.

She stared at the door, and he smiled at her. "You got it."

He nodded. "Yep. Let's see if it was worth the effort."

He swung the door open just as a bolt of lightning flared, a loud boom of thunder sounding at almost the same instant. Rain pounded the roof of the old church, and in seconds droplets of water began dripping into the building from the spotty old roof.

"We aren't going to stay dry long in here," Brynn commented, watching the drips slowly become rivulets.

Avery eased the door to the old iron safe open.

He took her flashlight and shined it inside. All that met their eyes was an ancient-looking stack of papers. "What is this?"

"It looks like financial records. Bank statements. Ledgers. Old credit card receipts." Avery shuffled through the stack.

"Why? What's important about them?" Brynn peered over his shoulder, shining the flashlight carefully at the stack.

Avery didn't answer at first. Then he cleared his throat. "Shadow Acres Retirement Home. It's that nursing home. Looks like that isn't all. Some other old houses that have been renovated into businesses. It looks like they're all tied to the same company that owns your birth parents' old house. Parham Holdings Company. Or District Attorney Clifford Parham. This doesn't look good."

"What? I don't understand. What does DA Parham have to do with my parents?" Brynn had a sinking feeling in the pit of her stomach. Whatever it was couldn't be good. Had they been in trouble of some sort? Tried to bribe the DA? She couldn't stomach asking the questions out loud.

"Unless I miss my guess, some of these records are forgeries from a nursing home. It looks like Parham Holdings and DA Parham were into some bad things."

Brynn still didn't understand. "Bad things like what?"

Avery looked up at her. Her eyes were wide

in the light of the flashlight. He didn't know how to tell Brynn how big this thing was. If he was right about what this meant, Suzanne Davis and her cronies were going to be the least of their worries.

THIRTEEN

"Major fraud and extortion."

She sucked in a breath.

He didn't have time to worry about it then, however. Before he could say anything else, a door slammed somewhere in the church building.

"What was that?" Brynn's eyes were round orbs as she faced him in the dim light.

"Who's there?" Avery called out. The only answer was a rumble of thunder that shook the building.

"Were we followed?" She turned her flashlight out into the dark hallway. Nothing but emptiness stared back. "You locked the door behind us, right?"

"Come on. Let's get out of here." Avery grasped her arm with one hand, the other clutching the files.

He didn't make it three steps before he heard it. It was a distant ticking noise. His adrenaline spiked and every hair on his body raised to attention.

"In here. Under the desk." He dragged Brynn into what looked like the old pastor's office. Inside, he led her to a doorway tucked into a nook at the back of the room. "How did you know this was here?"

"I saw it when we first came in." He turned on the light on his phone to illuminate a set of concrete steps leading into the basement. "Hurry!"

He closed the door and rushed down the stairs after her.

"What is it?" She was still trying to see what was going on.

"Explosives. Hear the ticking? Get down." Avery helped her take shelter under some old tables stored in the hollow space.

Her breathing was coming fast, but he had no time to think much about it. The blast shook the foundation above them, and debris flew around the room. The sickening sound of falling rocks filled his ears and timbers shook around them. When the hail of dust and debris began to settle, he raised his head from under the old table. The dark of the building couldn't hide the destruction. Sheetrock lay in splintered piles just a couple of yards away. The hall above them must have caved in. Piles of rock tumbled to-

ward them in a heap and rivulets of rain were
running into the crevices made from the edges
of the floor above, where it had once shielded
the rooms. There might not still be a roof on
the old church, he realized. It at least had some
holes in it.

"Are you okay?" He asked Brynn the question as he extended a hand to help her out from
under the makeshift shelter.

"I think so." She accepted his help and eased
out from beneath the table. When she saw his
view, however, a gasp slipped from her lips.

"It's destroyed." She raised the light again,
but it was just as bad as he had first thought.

"That might be the least of our worries." He
handed her the files. "Stay here for a moment.
If anything starts to collapse, get back under
that old oak table. It's the closest thing here to
bomb-proof."

She nodded her agreement and he slipped
up the steps toward the door. He pushed but it
didn't budge.

"This isn't good." He shoved at it again as
hard as he could. "Something's fallen up against
it."

"What do you mean? You can't get it open?"
Brynn stepped toward him.

He pushed again, and then again, but it wasn't
moving at all. She stepped up beside him and

tried to help, but it still didn't budge. "It looks like we're trapped."

Lightning flared and thunder shook the ground once more, punctuating his words.

Brynn's face paled when she reached to her pocket before remembering there was no cell service. "Oh no. We can figure something out, right? Surely we can knock the boards loose from the basement window or something."

"We can try." Avery moved over to the wall. "This window is still mostly intact. We'll have to be careful, or we'll end up in shreds from this old glass."

"Can we knock it out with something? There must be something heavy enough to do the job. A rock or something?" She gestured to the rubble against the wall. A beam lay across them and Sheetrock filled in the space leading to the hall. The steeple was above them, but it was in a tumbledown heap across the remainder of the roof.

"If we move too many things, that whole heap could come crashing down on us. It doesn't look very stable as it is." Avery eyed the pile suspiciously. It seemed to have imploded into the room. If the rocks hadn't been so heavy, they could have easily been hit by flying debris from the blast.

"So what do we do?" Brynn looked like she was struggling to stay calm.

Avery pondered her question, looking around at the destruction for another way out, when he caught a whiff of something that made his stomach turn over. Smoke.

She apparently smelled it, too. "Is the church on fire?"

"Looks like we don't have a choice. Stay back. I'm going to try to dislodge a stone large enough to break the window. It might collapse." Avery looked at her. "If it falls on me, promise me you'll take the stone and get out of here."

Their eyes met. He wanted to know she would be safe, no matter what happened to him.

The smell of smoke was getting stronger, and a haze began to float into the room, close to the roof. She shook her head. The heartbreak in her eyes matched the emotion he felt coursing through himself. "I'm not leaving you."

Tears welled in her luminous eyes. He had to make her see reason.

"Hopefully you won't have to. Just promise me that if I'm stuck, you'll try to get out. You can get help once you're safe." Avery gave her a stern look. "We don't have time to argue."

But he couldn't stop his own heart from jumping into his throat. He had just found her again. He couldn't bear the thought of losing her so soon.

Brynn had opened her mouth, probably to protest, but she shut it again at this last comment. "Just try not to get stuck, okay?"

She turned away, and though he knew it was probably to hide her own emotions, he was glad it kept her from seeing the turmoil he was in as well.

He gave a short laugh. "I'll do my best."

She backed away and he bent over the pile, searching for a stone that wasn't buried too deeply among the others. He found one sitting closer to the top and grasped it with both hands. When he tugged it free, the pile started to slide. He scrambled backward, but it settled again.

"That went better than I expected." He turned away with the stone.

A scraping, shuffling noise a second later brought him to attention.

"Avery, watch out!" Brynn grasped his arm and pulled him back as the pile began to slide once more. She coughed and he could see the smoke getting thicker, even in the dark. Lightning flared off and on from outside the small basement window, making the room look like a scene from a scary movie. He told her to try to keep her nose and mouth covered.

The pile of rubble skidded and then settled,

skidded and settled again. "We've got to hurry. The whole thing could collapse any moment."

Avery raised the stone, making sure Brynn was far enough back, and hit the glass hard. Red, blue and green glass splintered into panels and fell in the floor and the crevice between the window and the boards. He struck at the remaining shards along the edges of the frame and watched them fall as well.

The boards wouldn't be so easy, however. With the exterior made of stone, the window boards would have to be firmly anchored in with some sort of high-powered nail gun or drill. They weren't just going to pop loose.

Brynn coughed again behind him, and he felt the sting from the smoke as well. It lent a sense of urgency to his actions, the adrenaline spike giving him a boost in strength as well. He hammered at the corners in the top of the window first. If he could dislodge those, maybe the board would fall away.

He hammered relentlessly at it, though, with little success. Brynn was coughing more now, and he began to cough as well. The exertion required deeper breaths, and though he had pulled his shirt over his nose, the smoke was getting to him as well. Sweat pooled on his face and his shirt was damp. The wound in his shoulder was screaming in pain from his efforts. His back and arm muscles ached from the workout he was getting.

"It isn't working, is it?" Brynn had pulled her shirt from her nose to ask the question. He could hear the panic in her voice.

"Not yet. But I'm not giving up." He wanted to rest, but he didn't dare. There was no time for that. Surely he could get the board to break loose if he kept trying.

He hammered away, only an occasional wiggle indicating there was progress. His heart thudded from urgency and exertion. He couldn't keep this up much longer. He had to try something else, and fast.

Before he could come up with a plan, however, Brynn slid to the floor. "I'm so tired." She mumbled the words, her shirt sliding down away from her nose as she flopped down.

"No, Brynn, don't lie down." He stopped hammering at the board to turn to her. His stomach clenched. He had to keep her alert. "Stay with me. Get up."

"I can't." She groaned the words. "No energy."

He had to do something fast. He set the stone down at his feet. Pulling out his Glock, he shot right through the center of the board, squinting to protect his eyes the best he could. Satisfaction filled him when he saw the hole. Fresh air flowed in. He should have done that sooner.

Taking up the rock again, he hammered at the newly splintered hole in the board, breaking the plywood from the center. He finally had a large enough opening to push the board free enough to get them out.

"Brynn, come on. We're out!"

No answer came, though. When he turned around, she lay slumped on the floor.

She was unconscious.

An oxygen mask covered her face when Brynn awoke, and she felt more than mildly disoriented. Bright lights stung her eyes. She tried to focus, but she didn't remember how she got here, on a gurney in the back of an ambulance. Where was Avery?

Pieces of memories began to drift to her. The church. The explosion. Avery trying to get them out.

The file.

What had happened to the file and the evidence? Had Avery been able to get it out or was it still in the church? She tried to get up. She had to see what was going on.

"Whoa, stay put, there, little lady." A burly-looking EMT spoke, coming around from behind her head. "You've had a nasty bit of smoke inhalation. Gotta get those lungs cleared."

"Where's Avery?" Her throat ached from the smoke and her voice came out hoarse.

"He's getting some oxygen himself. Sounds like he dragged you out through a window. You both got pretty close to a serious incident back there." The EMT was shaking his head as if he was reprimanding her.

Thunder and lightning still put on a show beyond the ambulance windows.

She groaned, her whole body aching. "Tell me I'm not going to have to go to the hospital again."

"That's up to you. I don't think you sustained any serious injuries, and some oxygen and rest will usually suffice for the smoke." He patted her on the shoulder.

Relief filled her. Soon she could be out of here and back to the safe house to rest.

Concern about the files crept in again, though, and she wondered about the fate of the church. Flashing red lights glanced off the windows, and she wondered if firefighters were on the scene as well.

"Did they get the fire put out?" Brynn immediately regretted talking again, but she had to know.

"Still fighting it, last I knew. It'll be a total loss, anyway, what with the explosion." He adjusted a tube on the IV in her arm. "Shame about that old church. It was some cool old architecture. Not many left like that anymore."

Brynn nodded agreement, not willing to go through the pain of speaking again yet. Her thoughts were focused on the files. If Avery had pulled her through the window, there was no way he could have gotten the files out, too. Had they gone up in smoke?

If she hadn't been attached to the IV and oxygen, she would have been pacing. How could they prove the DA was involved and avenge her parents' deaths without those files? Was there any chance they might still be intact?

No, even if they hadn't burned, the water from the fire hoses would have destroyed the documents. How was she going to prove what happened?

She wasn't even sure of the details herself.

By the time she saw Avery again, he looked better than ever, even after what they had been through. Maybe that was her heart talking. "Ready to get going?" he asked.

Brynn raised herself up on her hands. "What, no police questioning this time?"

"I've already talked to them." He held out a hand to her and she took it, trembling a little.

"I thought you were getting oxygen," she said.

"I did. But that didn't take long. I spoke to the officer while they were finishing up the treatment." He looked at the EMT, who had just taken out her IV and bandaged her arm. "Is she free to go?"

He gave Avery the affirmative. Brynn stood, waited for the dizziness to pass, and followed Avery to Wilder's truck.

"Where's Wilder?" Brynn looked around, just realizing he was gone.

"His partner showed up on the scene and he went back to the precinct with him." Avery helped her into the truck.

"I wish we had been able to get the file out of the church." Brynn couldn't wait to get his ideas on what to do next.

"Do you mean that file?" He gestured toward the back seat.

She turned to see it lying in the seat. A gasp escaped. Then she coughed. "How? The EMT said you pulled me out of the church. You couldn't have held on to it, could you?"

He waited when she began to cough again. "I went back in for it."

"You did what?" Brynn felt anger flood her. "That was too dangerous."

"We need the proof. It seems like your mother went to a great deal of trouble to preserve that file and see to it that someone found it. I thought it was worth saving." Avery laid a hand on her cheek.

Tenderness flooded her, overtaking her anger. "That was too much. I appreciate it, but I'm sure we would have found another way. I never would have asked you to risk your life for it."

"It was nothing." Avery said the words as a means of dismissal. But it wasn't "nothing" to Brynn. She wanted to hug him.

Instead, she pulled the file into her lap and began looking through it. "What did the officer say when you told him about this?"

"I didn't tell him. If this is legit, we're going to have to come up with a plan. We can't just waltz in and accuse the district attorney of fraud and conspiracy. He seems to have some dirty cops in his pocket as well. And I know you think this proves it, but we don't actually have any evidence that he murdered your parents."

"What if he had someone else do it? Will we ever be able to link it back to him?" Disappointment and anger rippled through her. What if he got away with it?

"I need to talk to some people. Come up with a solid plan. Until then, we need to keep it quiet. If the Parhams learn we have this, they will come after us themselves."

"So you think this is what they were hiding? This is why Suzanne Davis came after me? But what does she have to do with it?" Brynn could think of plenty of possibilities, but none that she knew to be absolute.

"We need to find that out as well." Avery pulled into the safe house driveway and Brynn closed the file. She tucked it under her arm as she got out. Thankfully, the rain had stopped while she was in the ambulance and now the air smelled fresh and crisp.

It was getting late. She looked down to step over a puddle, but the soft click of the hammer being pulled back on a pistol stopped her in her tracks.

She looked up to see a man dressed in dark clothing aiming a pistol at her head. A subtle glance proved another guy had a gun on Avery as well. The first guy clicked his tongue, then whistled low.

"You found it." He pointed to the folder. "Boss will be pleased. Now we can clean up the mess."

FOURTEEN

Whatever mess the guy referred to couldn't be good. Avery assessed the situation. There was no way they would get out of this easily with two hit men holding guns on them.

And so much for keeping the file a secret.

He should have hidden it in the car until they knew what to do with it.

"We better take them to him as he said. File or no file, he's going to want to make sure they are eliminated, especially now that they've seen it. He doesn't take chances."

The man with the gun on Avery was speaking. He sounded a little more cultured than the other guy. Who were they, anyway? Their faces were covered, so Avery couldn't make out any features. But the sound of this guy's voice made him wonder if he was someone working for the DA in a more official capacity. He didn't sound like the typical hired goon.

"Fine. Let's go. Back in the car." They forced

them to get in, Brynn in the back seat with the hit man holding her hostage, and the cultured guy sitting up front in the passenger seat with better access to Avery.

She glanced at him, but he gave her a grim look. "Just do what they tell you."

He said it softly, but her eyes filled. He knew she was likely frustrated as well as frightened. They had been so close.

Had he botched this case as well? The idea that he had let Brynn down made him feel worse than he had ever felt. How had he gotten them into this?

But no, Avery wasn't through fighting yet.

His thoughts returned to what Brynn had told him about trusting him, even after all she had been through. She believed in him. She saw him as a hero. He couldn't let her down.

Now, however, wasn't the time to do anything rash. He would let these guys take them to their boss, see if it was indeed one of the Parham brothers, and work out a plan as they went. An opportunity would surely arise somewhere along the way. At least, he prayed it would. If it didn't, he would make one. He owed Brynn that.

His thoughts went to Wilder. His friend knew almost everything that was going on. Avery had shared so many of the details with him. Would he put the facts together and come looking for them? But he had no idea the DA was involved. And did the DA know Wilder was helping them? Wilder hadn't seen the file.

Avery was just going to have to come up with a plan himself. They couldn't rely on anyone else to know what was going on. It was up to him.

He thought he noticed the man in the back seat with Brynn texting with one hand while holding the gun on her with the other. Her breathing was fast, and she was still coughing occasionally from the smoke inhalation.

They drove to an old house just outside of town. It looked to have been built around the same time as the old house of Brynn's birth parents, but it was in much worse condition. It was crumbling and seemed to have been forgotten in every way. There were no other houses within shouting distance, and Avery could easily guess why they'd been brought here.

But when the men forced them inside, they tied them to an old iron stair railing and left.

"That's odd." Brynn coughed out the words.

"What's odd is they didn't gag us so we couldn't talk. They must not be planning on being gone long." Avery tugged fruitlessly at his restraints. "My guess is they're awaiting orders from the boss. Maybe he's on his way."

"What do you think these guys' obsession is

with old buildings?" Brynn looked around the house and shivered. "This one reminds me a lot of Cargill House, where I was adopted."

Avery was about to dismiss the comment until a thought occurred to him. "That's the connection. It must be. Suzanne Davis. The adoption agency. I bet if we looked into it, Parham Holdings would be the owner of Cargill House. They probably even made a great deal of cash from arranging your adoption. No wonder Suzanne Davis didn't want you to find out anything about it."

"Do you think that's why they saved me? At the time, they probably thought a baby wasn't any kind of threat. Just the opposite. If they owned an adoption agency, they probably decided they might as well make money off me in the bargain." Brynn sounded disgusted. He couldn't blame her.

"You're probably right. If they carried you out first, then staged it to look like your parents were trying to escape but your father had already rescued you, then no one would look too deeply into things. In fact, they made sure of it. And Suzanne Davis probably got paid a large chunk of money for her silence." Avery was having no trouble putting the pieces together now. "The DA could easily make sure the investigation was shut down quickly."

"And obviously they knew my birth mother had the file. The question is, how did she get it?" Brynn shrugged in her bindings, trying to alleviate some of her discomfort.

"That is a tough one. We'll figure it all out, though, once we get out of here." He mentally added an *if* to the statement. She needed him to be confident, though. He wouldn't add worry to her already shaken state.

"I wonder how the church all came to be a part of the equation. And why did the Realtor send us there? Also, how did the combination to the lock get on the picture? Did my parents add that before their death?" Brynn's mind was clearly working overtime.

"Maybe the documents in the safety deposit box can answer that question for us. I don't think the will was the only thing there. I can't help being suspicious about the banker who knew Rebecca Carrington wanting you to leave them. I wish we hadn't. And I am just as baffled as you are about the Realtor. Unless she set us up." Avery could think of no other reason Samantha Barnes would have sent them to the church.

They didn't have any more time to ponder it, however, for the hit men came back in. "Boss isn't inclined to interrupt his beauty sleep to deal with you two right now. I guess you'll just have to sleep here until morning. Maybe it'll be a good opportunity for you to think about all the things you wish you would have done before he kills you."

"Don't get any ideas, though." The cultured man added his own admonitions. "We'll still be standing guard."

The two men disappeared again, talking about mundane things as they walked out the door. Avery and Brynn were thrown into darkness once more.

"Well, it's obvious that sleep is out of the question." Brynn joked, groaning as she pulled at her bindings again. The stair rails held them upright with their backs against the hard iron railing. It cut into them where it twisted and gnarled decoratively.

"We're going to find a way to get out of here." Avery told her. "I doubt they will really be standing guard. They just want us to think they are. Those two buffoons are probably headed out to take a nap or something."

Their hands were tied up with some type of nylon ropes. They were slippery to a point, but the knots in them were solid. The worst part was that they were thin and bit into the wrist fiercely if a person pulled against them. He wasn't sure how to get out of them, but he would chafe his wrists completely raw to get away from them if he had to. He was going to get Brynn out of here.

"Avery, I'm sorry I got you into all this." Brynn's voice was soft beside him. "I want you to know I feel bad about it."

"Well, don't." He wasn't about to indulge her end-of-the-world ideas right now. He wanted to keep her mentally strong. He was more than willing to let her break down in his arms once they were safe. "We're going to get out of this, and it will be the greatest mystery we've ever solved. Maybe I'll even talk you into coming to work for me."

She gave a short laugh. Well, it was supposed to be a laugh. "Don't tease me, Avery. I really meant it. If anything happens to you… Well, I—I don't know what I'll do."

He swallowed hard. He felt the same way. He wanted to tell her so, but what if she lost it on him before he could save her? He couldn't take the risk, could he?

"I mean it. Like Sherlock and Watson. You'll get that proof and see your birth parents' deaths brought to justice. Promise me that. Otherwise, what are we fighting for?" He tried for sternness, but even he heard the slight quaver in his voice. It wasn't fear, he told himself. Well, if it was, it was for her, not himself. He was frustrated and anxious to get her out of here.

He couldn't—even in this dire situation—admit that he felt something for her that he had never felt before. That would make him weak. He needed to be strong this time. Not like with Selena. He had to get Brynn out of this, and in the process maybe he would remember that not all women were like Selena. Maybe.

As if she had read his mind, she spoke quietly into the darkness. "You never told me what really happened. I mean, to make you not want to fall in love again."

He sucked in a breath. "Her name was Selena. She worked for the US Marshals Service, and she was supposed to be helping me with a case. But she was beautiful, and that was her downfall. She used it to get close to people and work a case. I knew it, but somehow, I fell under her spell and believed she was in love with me. After all, we were supposed to be on the same side. But she turned out to be an informant. Her job with the Marshals Service was a cover. She was helping me find just enough information to lead her people to what they needed and then she turned on me. She almost got me killed in an ambush before we finally nailed her as the mole and took her into custody. It was the hardest thing I've ever had to do, turning someone in that I had fallen for. But she wasn't really who I thought she was. I had fallen in love with a fictional character she had created because she knew what I wanted. She had certainly done her research. She played me in the worst sort of way."

Brynn took his hand. "I'm so sorry. That must have hurt you deeply."

He made a sound of agreement, not sure what to say next. "You're different. I know that now. But I can't let my feelings get in the way when it comes to a case. I should never have let my heart get involved."

He was referring to both Selena and Brynn, but he didn't want to say so. He didn't want her to give up right now. They had to get out of this alive.

Brynn sucked in a breath. "I thought so, too, at first. But then I realized that if your heart is never involved, life isn't really worth living. I used to think I was in love with you when we were in school. I was wrong. I just had a crush."

When she paused, Avery felt a harsh stab of disappointment. Did he want her to be in love with him? The answer was a resounding yes. So when she continued, he was speechless.

"However, now that I really know you, I know the difference between having a crush and loving someone. And I love you. Whether you ever return those feelings or not, there they are." Brynn's voice cracked then.

Avery breathed in and out. He didn't know

what to say. In an instant, he knew the truth. He loved her, too. He couldn't help it.

"Brynn, I—"

"Don't, Avery. Don't say you love me just because I said I loved you. I just wanted you to know in case we don't make it. I wanted you to know you are loved." Brynn was crying now: he could hear it in her voice.

He didn't know if he could tell her. He didn't know if admitting his feelings for her would ruin it for them both.

But what if they didn't make it out of here alive? She should know.

"We're going to make it. Do you hear me?" He drew in a breath. "I do love you. And we will figure it all out once this is over.

She sucked in a breath. Was she afraid he didn't mean it? He spoke again. "I'll prove it to you."

Avery waited for his words to sink in. But he could only wait so long. They had to get out of here.

He said so aloud. "If we put our heads together we can come up with a plan."

"What did they do with the file?" Brynn sounded weary. That wasn't what he wanted, but he knew she would probably need some time to see he meant his words.

"They left it here. I saw the taller guy lay it

on a table near the entry. I hope he forgot about it. Maybe he just thought he would leave it for the boss." He spoke quietly in case they really were outside. "I don't know if they mean the DA or his brother. Either way, we will nab it on our way out."

"And how do we figure out just how to get out of here?" He could hear her squirming uncomfortably against the ropes once more.

"Honestly, it's a little hard to come up with a good plan when someone is questioning you incessantly." He tried to sound serious, but his tone gave him away.

"Oh, really? I thought maybe you needed some help thinking. If I don't question you, how will you ever spark an idea?"

He liked that she always gave his teasing right back to him. "I probably wouldn't. But if I did, I would be sure to lose it in all the questions. You switch gears like no one I've ever seen."

"Tell me what to do. I can't stand just waiting." Brynn huffed out a breath beside him.

"If I knew yet, I would. Obviously we have both tried pulling and tugging to loosen them. I'm not sure what to try next." Avery was currently working his bonds back and forth against the iron of the stair railing, hoping to wear it thin.

It wasn't working.

* * *

Brynn listened for a moment, figuring out what he was doing. "That could work, but it's going to take too long."

"And do you have a better idea?" he asked.

"Maybe so." She shifted her weight beside him.

"Well, don't be shy. What is it?" Avery kept sawing. Apparently he wasn't going to chance putting too much stock in her plan just yet.

"When the door opened, enough light came in to reflect off something shiny on the floor. I made sure to look more closely when they opened the door again. I think it's a shard of glass." Brynn was scooting lower and trying to stretch her bound hands out behind her to gain some length.

"That's great, but how do we get it?" Avery didn't sound impressed with her findings.

"I think I can reach it with my feet. So I only need to figure out how to get it from the ground to my hands." Brynn wriggled and inched her feet toward her prize.

"And then what? You can't bend down to get it." Avery watched dubiously.

"They didn't tie my ankles so well." As she reached the shard of glass and slid it toward herself, she gave her legs a hard jerk and the ties broke loose.

"Okay. Nice. But I still don't see how you're going to cut our hands free with it." Avery kept watching what he could make out of her efforts in the darkness.

Brynn kicked out of her shoes and carefully peeled off a sock with her other foot, hooking it with her toes. It took a couple of tries, but once she had one foot bare, she carefully plucked up the glass shard between her toes.

"Ouch!" She sucked in a breath.

"Brynn, I don't know what you're doing, but—"

"Just trust me a moment." She didn't mean to sound testy, but she needed to concentrate.

It was apparent the glass would be sharp enough to cut their bonds, so she scooted carefully back to an upright position. Her hands were tied to a low part of the stair rail behind her, so she thought if she could be careful enough, she might be able to reach behind her to cut the ropes on her wrists.

As long as she could avoid slitting her wrists in the process.

Working carefully to grasp the glass between her toes, she bent her leg backward at the knee, twisting her ankle inward toward her bound hands. Using one hand to guide it when she had brought her foot close, she fixed the glass against the rope. Once it was there, she gave her leg a quick downward jerk.

"You have some unique skills," Avery commented wryly.

"Ballet as a child. Yoga as an adult. It really improves flexibility."

It slipped at the last second, however, and the glass clattered back to the floor.

"Did it work?" Avery sounded doubtful.

"No. I dropped the glass. But I'm going to try again." Already she was working the shard of glass back into position between her toes. She had been relieved to find it hadn't gone far when it fell from between them to the floor.

This time she made sure to grip it tightly with her toes as she jerked it through the rope. A soft ripping sound was all the evidence she needed that she had done some good this time. A good tug ripped it the rest of the way lose. However, the glass also ripped into the tender flesh of her toes.

She let out a gasp.

"Are you okay?" Avery's voice was full of concern.

Her response was to show him what was left of her bonds. She held them close so he could see them in the dark. She kept her voice to an excited whisper. "I'm better than okay. I'm free."

She gripped the glass shard and leaned in behind Avery to cut him free as well.

"Let's get out of here." He flexed his wrists, whispering.

Brynn grabbed her shoes and her discarded sock as Avery dove toward the shelf to grab the file. "Watch the glass. I think it's from a broken mirror. Whatever it is, it'll make a lot of noise if you step on it."

"Let's try the back door." Avery led the way. He paused to look out, trying to locate the guard their captors had promised.

"Do you see anyone?" Brynn leaned close, ignoring her burning toes. Warmth oozed from between them with every step, and she worried she would leave a trail from the bleeding.

"Not yet. Put your shoes back on. We're going to have to run for it." Avery moved to another window to look out at a new angle.

Once Brynn had her shoes back on, she raised up from her crouched position to try to see around him again. "There. Is that something moving over by that tree?"

Avery checked out the area she indicated. "I think so. We need to create a distraction."

The men had taken their cell phones and tossed them when they had tied Brynn and Avery up, so they couldn't call for help. The best they could do was run for it and try to get help.

"Do you have any ideas?" Brynn didn't. She couldn't think of anything that wouldn't just draw more attention back to them.

"I'm going to check the front." Avery gestured for her to stay put. At least, that was what Brynn assumed it meant.

She kept watching the spot by the tree, but she saw no more movement. Was he sleeping? If so, that could work to their advantage.

She was about to say something about it in a loud whisper to Avery when he came creeping quietly back to her. "I don't think there is a guard out front. We can probably make a break for it before anyone notices."

"Perfect. I think the guard around back is asleep, too." Brynn pointed out the window. "Can we be quiet enough to get out?"

"We're sure gonna give it a try." Avery motioned for her to follow.

They eased open the door, waiting a moment to see if anyone appeared. When no one did, they stepped out onto the porch. The moon provided just enough light for them to see a path down the steps and across the lawn. An occasional cloud scuttled by, temporarily blotting out some of their light as they made their way hurriedly on the grass. An owl hooted a few yards away, and Brynn sucked in a breath to keep from reacting.

She was just about to sigh with relief as they made it to the street and across to a stand of trees, when a shout of warning sent a cold dread pulsing through her.

"Run!" Avery commanded.

He led her toward the trees, and they stumbled into the thin cover. It wouldn't be enough to hide them, but maybe enough of a shield to slow their pursuers down a bit.

Avery crammed the folder into his jacket and zipped it up tight as he waited for her to catch up. When she did, he grasped her hand and led her through the trees.

There weren't many occupied homes within easy running distance. The late hour ensured no one was out and stirring. It was so quiet it was eerie. Not even a dog's bark sounded in the rural area; it was just the crunch of their running feet and an occasional snapping twig.

She could hear their pursuer yelling at someone as he came dashing after them. She didn't make out much other than anger and a few curse words. She sure didn't turn to see if he was alone or not.

She was terribly out of breath from being dragged along behind Avery's much faster form, but she could see the edge of the tree line ahead of them. Hopefully, that meant she would have an easier time of it. The tree roots and brush in the woods were hard to navigate, forcing her to pick her feet up higher and step over natural obstacles. She sagged with relief.

But her relief was premature. She looked up at Avery for a split second as he glanced back to urge her on. When she did, her ankle caught in a snag of brush and tree roots protruding from the ground. Her foot wrenched painfully away from her leg, twisting her ankle at a nasty angle. She stumbled and fell, jerking her hand from Avery's grasp. She tried to jump to her feet, but pain forced her down once more, and she fell, crying out.

Avery paused to come back to her, but the slick ticking of a gun being cocked froze him where he stood.

"Leave her where she is. Boss wants her alive. You, however, he couldn't really care less about."

Even in the dark, she could see the evil gleam in their captor's eyes.

FIFTEEN

Avery wanted to lunge at the man. There was no way he would die and leave Brynn at this man's mercy. He waited, though, knowing a more opportune time would come. He looked from Brynn, lying on the ground gripping her ankle, to the man holding the gun. They were at a serious disadvantage at the moment.

"She's hurt. Can I at least look at her ankle?" It would buy him some time.

The heartless man had the gall to shrug. "Boss doesn't care about her ankle. He's going to end up killing her either way. Where's the file?"

Ah. He had almost forgotten, but there was his advantage. "What file?"

Their captor roared back at him. "I know one of you has it. Don't play stupid. Boss is gonna have to see that file destroyed with his own eyes. Where is it?"

Anger issues, Avery thought, would definitely

work to his favor. He would try to annoy the man a little more to see if he could get him to slip up and do something dumb.

Just not too dumb. He had to keep Brynn safe.

"Oh, we hid that before we left." Avery sighed. "I thought it'd be easier to come back for it. Did you have a nice nap?"

Just as he had figured, the man began to curse and rushed at Avery. When he did, he made the mistake of lowering the gun. Avery dodged him and quickly turned and slipped the file from his jacket while the man was seeing the haze of red anger, hoping Brynn would get to it first.

Avery steeled himself against the bigger man, kicking the gun out of his grasp. It went off, but the bullet glanced off a tree in the distance. Avery laid into him, blocking a meaty fist before landing a solid punch to the man's throat. While he gurgled in pain, Avery struck out again, a solid blow to his jaw this time. When his head shot back, he roared in pain, coming at Avery again with his solid fists.

Avery ducked the first blow, but the second glanced off his cheek, sending sparks of pain shooting through his head. He reeled a moment before sending a hard fist to the man's midsection. He turned then and thrust an elbow into his captor and then turned into him with a sharp knee. When the bigger man started sucking in air, he shoved the heel of his hand into the man's nose and then swept a foot out from under him as his nose spurted blood. Avery jumped on him, trying to get leverage. The goon outweighed Avery, at almost double his body weight, but Avery was much quicker. If he could keep that advantage, the man couldn't overpower him.

But the big man struggled and rolled Avery, blood still oozing from his nose all the while. Avery could see the man blinking tears from his eyes as he tried to get a good hold on Avery, who kept rolling and ducking away just in time.

Avery laid another fierce punch into the man's midsection, knocking the wind out of him and gaining the advantage once more. He straddled the thug, holding him down with his weight. He kept landing blows, hoping he was making some sort of progress at putting the man into a stupor, not noticing that Brynn had been quietly crawling over to the gun he had kicked from the man's hand. She had tucked the file away and stood over them holding the gun.

"Stop!" She shouted the words with an assertion Avery didn't know she possessed. She held the gun close to the man's head, steady-handed and calm.

The man looked up in fear and confusion, clearly disoriented from the punches Avery had landed to his head. He slowly raised his hands. "Do you even know how to shoot that thing?"

"Trust me, she does." Avery leaned on the man's chest to help hold him down and then searched for something to tie him with. He finally settled for the string out of the hood of his jacket, jerking it free with a slight ripping sound.

He tied the man securely, wrapping the strings around his wrists several times before knotting them, but knowing it wouldn't last, he looked to Brynn. "We need something better to secure him with. We can't have him running back to the house to meet his coconspirators."

Brynn thought, then offered her jacket. "Maybe you could use the long sleeves to wrap around him and tie his arms close to his body like a straitjacket or something."

"It will help." Avery took it and did as she suggested, the small jacket barely reaching around the large man.

"You aren't going to get away with this. Bruce will be looking for you. For all of us. He's probably back by now." The man was sputtering like a toddler now.

Avery wiped his face and mouth where blood was running down in rivulets.

"Actually, I might have an idea about that."

Avery looked at her before pulling out the man's cell phone.

"You can't open it." The man sounded much like a junior high bully taunting a playmate.

Avery held it up to the man's face. Even in the low lighting, it opened right up. "Might as well just tell me the passcode."

Avery went to the last text he had sent, reporting them gone. The response to it was scathing. Avery typed a new message to tell Bruce the captives were recovered. A quick reply came back.

GOOD. NOW MAYBE I WON'T HAVE TO WATCH BOSS KILL YOU.

"What're you doing?" The big man was still protesting.

"Nothing you need to worry about." Avery saw that Brynn was simply watching him silently, and he remembered her ankle.

"Are you okay?" His voice was gentle, more than he had intended, but he couldn't help it. She brought out too many feelings of tenderness in him.

"Yes. I will be. The pain is already easing up. What now?" She still held the gun on their captive, her eyes watching him carefully between glances at Avery.

"We're going to set a trap." Avery replied.

He dialed in Wilder's number. Within a few minutes he had told his friend everything, from the files to their capture and escape. They made a plan to set up as if Avery and Brynn were still captives and get the "boss" to talk. Wilder would be hiding with his team to take him down once they did.

"It'll never work!" Beefy Fists was still trying to interject his opinion when Avery disconnected. "What will you do if they call and want to talk to me? And don't you think they'll miss me?"

Avery wanted to roll his eyes. "Well, you see, if you'll agree to cooperate, Wilder is going to make sure you get a good deal, rather than going to prison for a very long time. But if not, we'll leave you tied up out here in the woods and hope nothing has tried to eat you before we come back."

The man's eyes widened. "Eat me? There's nothing out here that could do that."

"Isn't there? You aren't from this area, then, are you? Coyotes, wolves, bears and mountain lions have all been seen in this area, quite often actually." Avery shrugged. "If you were well armed and had your limbs free you might be okay. But you won't be."

The man started to talk then. "Other than

Bruce, you have Suzanne and Davy to contend with. Then there is the boss and his brother. They'll be here at first light. How do you plan to get them all?"

"Let me worry about those details. You have a part to play," Avery growled. "Who is coming in the morning? Your boss?"

"Yes. And he'll expect Bruce and me to be here."

"And his brother? Will he be with him? What part does he play in all this?" Avery knew he had to be talking about the DA and his brother, but he wasn't sure which one was the boss.

"I don't know. He stays to the shadows most of the time. Tries to keep up his public image and all. He mostly keeps us all out of trouble."

Maybe he had that figured wrong. If the DA wasn't in charge, this might not work. He needed the man to confess.

"What public image?" Brynn spoke up.

The man's eyes widened as if just realizing what he'd said. Then he sighed. "I guess you're gonna find out anyway. Boss's brother is the DA."

"The DA isn't in charge? Of Parham Holdings?" Avery asked this question.

"They're partners, I suppose. But the DA tries to keep his nose clean, you know, let little brother handle all the shady stuff."

"Except for swindling people out of money and covering up arson." Brynn's voice was full of sarcasm.

They had begun walking back toward the house, Avery explaining the plan to Brynn as they went. He took over the gun, holding it on their captive as they went.

Avery watched their surroundings, holding a finger on their captive's phone screen so he could keep it open. He didn't call the local authorities because he didn't want them to alert the DA to what was happening. Someone was keeping him informed from the inside.

"There'll be a sniper on you, just so you know. If you decide not to cooperate, you'll be the first casualty," Avery began to explain to the man. "A SWAT team will be in place. It turns out Wilder has made friends in higher-ranking law enforcement offices than just the Cheyenne police force."

Brynn made a noise of relief. "They'll be in place by the time his boss shows up?"

"They're already on their way." Avery had barely begun to tell Wilder what all was going on when his friend had determined it was time to get the FBI involved. It seemed he had a close female friend with the feds.

Avery didn't have time to ponder the nature of Wilder's relationship with her, however. He

was too busy planning their end of the take-
down. If this didn't work, they could all end up
getting killed. He had to focus.

They arrived back at the abandoned house,
making everything look normal before Wilder
and the team arrived to get things set up. They
found Bruce sleeping at his post and had him
secured and tied up in the shed with little effort.

When Wilder arrived, they found a closet
where the recorder could be hidden to get all
the information they needed. They would plant
some men inside to take the men down quickly.
Avery found a trapdoor to a basement hidden
in the walk-in pantry. It would make a perfect
place to keep the support team hidden.

The plan was to make it look like Avery and
Brynn were still secured, but they wouldn't actually be tied. He just hoped and prayed the men
wouldn't check their bonds too closely. If their
captive played his role well enough, they would
have no reason to suspect.

If he didn't, one signal from Avery would tell
them to take the guy out and go on the offensive.

He just had to keep the guy away from Brynn
so she stayed out of danger.

Brynn was nervous about Avery's plan.
She wanted to know everything about her parents' deaths and what had really happened, but

she knew there was a lot that could go wrong. He squeezed her hands occasionally to reassure her, but she could tell he was distracted.

She felt a surge of warmth for him. He had been so kind, so tender and sweet to her throughout all of this. She had to wonder if she was wrong to place him in the same category as the guys from her past. He seemed so different. It made her want to try a relationship again.

Her thoughts went to his confession of love for her. She wanted to believe him, and for a moment she had. But she was probably just being silly. He had explicitly told her he had no interest in a romantic relationship at all, and probably especially not with her. So she would just have to suppress whatever feelings she might have. She had known all along to keep her heart out of things. And though it might take time, she would eventually get over Avery Thorpe, right? At least, that was what she would tell herself.

By the time Avery and Wilder had the SWAT team in place, the first hint of sunlight was creeping up the eastern sky. Fatigue and sleepiness combined to tug at Brynn from top to toe and hunger rumbled in her middle.

She was still suppressing hunger pains when the low roar of an engine sounded outside the house. Arguing sounded among the slamming of doors just after it shut off. Brynn hoped that meant they would be too preoccupied to notice any signs of the ambush to come. Though Avery had been very careful, it was difficult to ensure they had covered everything in such a short period of time. A sudden shout cut off the chatter, and shortly after, the door to the house flew open. Brynn didn't have to do any acting to seem nervous and frightened. If this went awry, it could certainly end badly. She didn't want to consider the possible outcomes if things didn't go as planned.

A tall, silver-bearded man who could only be Jake Parham strode in with an air of authority. He looked like a heavier version of Clifford Parham, whom she had often seen in photos and on the news because of his DA status. Jake was followed by Suzanne Davis and a shorter man wearing a black toboggan.

"Where's the file?" The tall man didn't even spare them a glance.

Their captor, whose name they had learned was Eddie, nervously pointed him toward the folder full of papers. Parham snatched it up, flicking a Zippo lighter out of his pocket and snapping it open.

"What're you doing?" Suzanne Davis rushed forward. "Won't the DA want to see it destroyed?"

"He'll take my word for it." Parham struck

flint to lighter and held the flame to the edge before tossing the whole thing into the empty fireplace grate. Brynn gasped as the evidence her mother had worked so hard to secure went up in flames. Parham watched it burn for a moment before turning to the captives. He released a satisfied laugh.

"Now there is the messy part. Davy…" He gestured, and the man, who didn't fit his name in Brynn's opinion, pulled out a 9mm. His beefy hands and oversize, bearded form didn't go with the boyish name at all. He had a thick bandage around one thigh.

"Wait!" Brynn let the word burst from her lips as he pointed the gun at her. "Please. Before you kill me, I want to know about my birth parents. Why were they killed?"

Davy paused, his finger easing away from the trigger. He looked from Parham to Suzanne and then back to her.

"I have no idea what you're talking about." Parham snarled the words.

"I think you do." Brynn spoke the words quietly, but they resonated in the barren house. She didn't have to pretend to feel the sorrow that prompted tears to gather in her eyes.

There was a pause and Brynn's pulse throbbed in her ears as nervousness and fear swept through her. What would they do if he wouldn't talk?

"If you don't tell her, I will." Suzanne surprised Brynn with her low words.

"You won't be telling anything." Parham cut a vicious look in Suzanne's direction. "She can just assume they were as nosy as she is, and it got them killed. You're lucky to even be here."

"She deserves to know, Jake. You can give her that much. You're taking everything else from her." Suzanne sounded assertive, surprising Brynn with her boldness.

Parham's phone rang and he released an angry breath. "You're still too soft for this, Sue."

But he stepped away to answer the call.

Brynn took advantage of the moment. She appealed to Suzanne softly. "You knew who I was the first time you saw me. You knew my parents, didn't you?"

Suzanne stepped toward her, head down and eyes not quite meeting Brynn's own. "The Carringtons were nice people. I didn't really know Jake until after the Carringtons died. The Parhams owned the adoption agency I worked for, and Jake brought you to me. I hadn't been there long, and I'd just lost my husband to a boating accident. Jake offered me a big stack of cash to keep everything quiet. Of course, I needed the money desperately."

"The Parhams own Cargill House?" Brynn asked, although they had already put the facts together. It was an old property, like the others, and Parham Holdings had a variety of "human service" businesses, though she had surmised long ago the brothers were out to make money, rather than provide a helpful service.

"The Parhams own over half the county." Suzanne sounded annoyed by the fact.

"So if you had refused to arrange my adoption, you would have been out of a job. But how did you get further involved? Why didn't you take the cash Parham offered you and find work somewhere else?" Brynn was genuinely curious about this woman's story. It was obvious, even though she had threatened her on more than one occasion, that this woman was doing what she felt she had to do to survive.

"Because Jake Parham charmed me. He pretended to be interested in me personally. He made me promises he never intended to keep. He even convinced me to give my own child up for adoption. You see, I was pregnant when my husband died. Jake convinced me that my daughter and I would both be better off. What I didn't understand was how much money he would make from the arrangement." Suzanne's eyes filled with tears. "By the time I had him figured out, it was too late. Not only would he ruin me, but without the protection of Jake's brother, I would have spent my life in prison."

Brynn couldn't help feeling sympathetic toward Suzanne. Wasn't everyone just one bad decision in life away from creating chaos? But she still had questions. "But my parents knew too much. Is that why they were killed?"

Parham chose that moment to reenter the conversation. Brynn had been too engrossed in the ongoing talk with Suzanne to realize he had returned. "Your mother tried to spy on all of us. She wasn't a very good one. She got caught."

"What do you mean? I know nothing about the Carringtons." Brynn hoped this would be her opportunity to learn. She glanced toward Avery, but he remained silent, giving an almost imperceptible nod.

"Your mother was a good lawyer. But she was too concerned with things that she shouldn't have worried about. When she went to work in Clifford's offices, she should have stuck to doing her job and keeping her mouth shut. Instead, she got her husband involved." Jake Parham had apparently decided to talk.

"How did she get my father involved?" Brynn hadn't known her mother had worked with Parham and she didn't know much about what kind of lawyer her father been, either.

"He was a corporate lawyer. When she started talking, he decided to start investigating some things himself. He began to find evidence to compile against us." Parham shrugged as if it didn't matter.

"Evidence of what?" Avery had been very quiet until now, but he finally chose to speak up.

Parham seemed to realize what he was doing. He snorted. "I'm sure you looked through the file before you were captured."

"It looked like you were committing fraud in your billing department of the nursing homes. Is that correct?" Avery knew very well what it was, but he needed Parham to make the admission.

Parham rolled his eyes. "The insurance companies make it easy. But that wasn't all."

Before Jake Parham could continue, the door to the house opened again and this time the DA himself stepped in. "What's taking you so long? I thought this would be finished by now."

Jake Parham sent his brother a guilty look. "I kept getting calls."

"You couldn't have these nimrods just take care of it?" Clifford Parham gestured toward Davy and Eddie.

Jake muttered something in answer, but Clifford Parham had focused his attention on Brynn. "They weren't lying when they said you were the spitting image of Rebecca. It kind of takes me back thirty years. If she had just given up her stubborn pride and done what I asked, we wouldn't all be here right now."

Brynn jerked back as he trailed a finger over her cheek. "What does that mean?"

He grinned, but it made her feel slimy somehow. "I tried to get her to leave your father and run away with me. I was going to raise you as my own. But she wouldn't do it. Then I found out why. She was spying on me the whole time. Now it'll be like making her pay all over again."

Brynn shuddered. She couldn't imagine what her life would have been like had she been raised by this man. In a way her mother had died trying to protect her from such a fate.

"Never mind, Davy. You can put that Ruger away. I want to kill this one myself. It'll be almost as thrilling as setting fire to her parents' home with them inside." Cold fury filled Clifford Parham's eyes. "You know, I created a little gas leak in their home that evening just to be sure they wouldn't be coherent enough to get out alive."

Clifford Parham pulled his own 9mm from his waistband and in a millisecond, Avery gave a shout. He lunged free of his pretend bonds to knock Brynn out of the way as two shots went off.

SIXTEEN

A ricochet of bullets left the room in chaos.

Avery shielded Brynn beneath his own form, as they heard the noise of the SWAT team coming in to take control of the scene.

Avery hadn't wanted Brynn to see Parham's body, but it was far too close and he couldn't suffocate her forever. She had to be running out of air crushed beneath him. But before he could tell her to look the other way, however, she had seen.

Clifford Parham was the only casualty, thankfully. Though bullets had grazed some of Parham's cronies, none of them faced life-threatening injuries. Avery's stomach turned at the thought. It couldn't be helped. He wasn't about to take the chance on the man killing Brynn first, and he and Wilder had agreed that a sniper would be prepared to take anyone out who tried to hurt her. It had all been far too risky for Avery's comfort, but he was thankful it had ended.

Wilder approached now, and one of the members of the SWAT team gently led Brynn away. She was strong, not looking at Parham any longer, but still holding her head up and walking out with composure. He had seen some strong men crumple at such a scene.

"Did you get enough?" Avery asked Wilder then. "I'm sorry it wasn't all we had hoped for."

"It's enough. Besides, Davy and Eddie are gonna give up more than enough. They've already been trying to tell the FBI stuff no one even asked about yet." He chuckled. "Watching their protector get taken out seems to have really shaken them up."

"Perfect. And what about Suzanne Davis?" Avery looked toward the woman being taken away in handcuffs. She had surprised him.

"She'll take whatever deal she is offered. She honestly just seems to be glad it's all over. The poor woman really got trapped in a bad situation. Unfortunately, she still committed some crimes that she'll have to answer for." Wilder shook his head.

"I hope Brynn can get a chance to talk to her eventually. She'd love to learn more about her birth parents. There are still a lot of questions out there. Who knows if Jake Parham will ever answer them—for anyone."

"Probably not. But we can put most of the

pieces together with what we do have." Wilder clapped him on the shoulder. He offered Avery a set of car keys. "You need to get her home and let her get some rest. She's been through a lot."

They were walking out the door of the old abandoned house, and Avery caught sight of Brynn sitting on a gurney with a SWAT member standing beside her. He hadn't even heard the paramedics arrive, but it looked like they had already checked her over. Still, Brynn was pale, eyes wide as she looked up at him, their gazes making contact and holding.

His thoughts went to what would happen now. Was he about to lose her for good? Would she go back to Texas, never to return? Or would he see her on the rare occasion that she came to visit her aunt and he happened to bump into her around town? He couldn't stand to ponder either thought.

Reporters were arriving on the scene, however, and it was time to get her out of here. The last thing she needed was some news reporter hounding her for answers right now.

Brynn offered him a weak smile as he approached. "We did it. Right?"

He couldn't quite meet her eyes. "Yeah. I think so."

"Did the feds get what they needed? Or is it

going to hurt us that he destroyed the file?" She looked crestfallen at the thought.

"Oh, we still have the files. Maybe not physical files, but we have them." Avery finally looked her in the eye.

"What do you mean?" Brynn's brow furrowed.

"Wilder was able to digitally scan copies of everything while we were getting everything set. We knew Parham would destroy them as soon as he got his hands on them. So we covered all our bases." Avery glanced over his shoulder.

"What's wrong, then?" Brynn must have read his expression.

"The reporters are arriving. We need to get out of here." Avery jerked a thumb in the direction of the vehicles pulling down the drive.

"Ugh. Yes, please let's go, then." Brynn stood, wobbling slightly.

The paramedic nearby lunged for her. "Take it easy. Don't get in too big of a hurry."

She smiled at him. "I'm fine."

Avery led her away, and when they were headed away from the chaos now erupting on the morning scene, he asked her about what concerned him most. "So now that you learned what you needed to know, will you be going back to Texas?"

Her expression was inscrutable. "I still hope

to tie up a few loose ends, but yes. I guess I don't have a reason to stay any longer after that."

With everything in him, he wanted to give her a reason to stay right then. But he held back, not wanting to say something she wouldn't be ready to hear. Who was he kidding? He was just afraid of rejection—of learning that the tender emotions he had developed for her over the past several days weren't reciprocated. Or worse yet, they weren't enough for her to take a chance on him.

Better to just let her go. That way he wouldn't get hurt.

He tried to steer his thoughts to the conversation she had just begun. "What loose ends do you mean? Are you just hoping to learn more about your birth parents now that you know who they were?"

"Yes." She hesitated. "I'm hoping once everyone realizes there is no longer any threat from the Parham brothers, they'll open up a little more about it. I could be wrong, but I have to try."

"What about your aunt?" Avery kept walking and didn't look at her. She might not be willing to take a chance on him, but he was more than ready to take a chance on her. He tried to keep his eyes from straying to her lips. The memory of her kiss haunted him.

"I'll come back and visit her. And I'd love to learn how the file got into the church safe. I also wonder about my mother's prayer book. It was pretty interesting." Brynn still sounded exhausted, and Avery suddenly felt guilty for keeping her engaged.

"You know what? You need sleep. Let's talk about it tomorrow. I'll help you with anything you need. Right now, I need to get you back to the safe house." Avery grasped her hand and squeezed it.

But even after Brynn had gone to her room and fallen fast asleep, Avery's mind spun with thoughts of what the future held. Possibilities played out in his mind, though he tried his best to shut the scenarios out. Brynn's face haunted his every thought, however, and he finally gave up and let his mind drift to what might be.

Would she ever give up her job in Texas? Could she even love him? But a vision of Brynn in white teased him, smiling and reaching for him with her dainty hand.

He tried reminding himself of Selena. But there wasn't a single similarity between the two women, other than the fact that they were both females. Brynn was everything good and kind, and in a pang of realization, Avery realized he loved her with everything in him. He had thought he loved her before, but now he realized it was enough to move past his hurts. It wasn't at all like his feelings for Selena, but a real and lasting tenderness that would surpass any test that time might send their way. He loved her. There was no doubt about it.

The only question left in his mind now was what to do about it.

Brynn hadn't slept so hard in months, maybe longer. As soon as she woke up fully, though, her mind began to replay the events of the last several days. It made her groan, and she rose to go shower, but before she could get there, Avery saw her coming out of her room.

"I'm glad you got some rest." He told her after greeting her. "Once you feel up to it, I thought we'd head back to Corduroy so your aunt can have the reassurance of seeing you safe and sound. She and Camille have been frantic with worry."

"I'm sure. Aunt Martha didn't seem to believe me when I told her on the phone. She said my voice sounded weak and I'd better take care of myself." Brynn smiled to herself. Aunt Martha was sometimes a tad bossy with her. She liked to mother Brynn whenever she got the chance.

"Well, she wasn't wrong. You had a rough time, and it was becoming apparent. No offense, of course." Avery smiled at her, but there was some intensity in his blue eyes that told her there was more on his mind than what he was saying.

"No offense, huh? It isn't exactly flattering." She ran a hand through her wild hair self-consciously. Was that why he was staring at her like that? She felt her face flame. "I really need to shower and change."

"Of course." He stepped back, but he didn't turn, just kept watching her as she went into the bathroom. What was that all about?

But even on the drive back to Corduroy, he never said anything to indicate what he was preoccupied with. He did keep giving her that odd look from time to time, though.

When they returned to Camille's B and B, Aunt Martha wrapped Brynn in a hug and wouldn't release her for several seconds. Brynn told the two women the whole story while Avery listened, inserting an occasional nod or murmur of agreement.

"I'm so glad you're okay. I told your father you would ask questions one day. He told me we had to leave it in the Lord's hands." She squeezed Brynn's hand. "I'm so glad it's all over and you're safe."

Brynn looked at Aunt Martha in surprise. Her adoptive father, Blake Evans, had been Aunt Martha's brother. It wasn't a surprise that she talked to him about it. But the idea that he was suspicious about her birth parents' past in any way was a shock.

"What do you mean? My father knew?"

Aunt Martha glanced at Avery. "He started to figure out who your birth parents had been a few years before they moved you to Texas. He kept your mother—Stephanie, your adoptive mother—pretty well in the dark about it. I didn't know the real reason for Blake and Stephanie's move for a long time. I doubt that Stephanie ever really questioned it. She hadn't really known the Carringtons. But Blake did at one time."

"You knew as well?" Brynn was still trying to process all of this.

"Not everything. Blake made sure of that. And if his warnings weren't enough to convince me of the danger, his death certainly was." She teared up. "It was difficult, living with my suspicion that his death hadn't truly been an accident. But it was obvious whoever was behind all of it wouldn't hesitate to kill anyone they thought might interfere. I wanted to warn you as soon as I understood what you were up to. But I didn't dare let on that I knew anything. And I prayed you would figure the whole thing out and not get hurt. Once I learned you had Avery

Thorpe on your side, I felt confident you two could do it."

Brynn nodded. "I'm glad you didn't put yourself in danger. But I never knew Dad's death wasn't an accident."

Aunt Martha settled into a plush sage green armchair. "I never had any proof. But after everything that had already happened, in my heart, I knew. I hoped you'd be the one to end it all and bring some closure, though I had no idea how you'd put the pieces together. You're a smart young lady."

"I had a lot of help from Avery. Though we almost didn't figure it out ourselves." Brynn smiled at her aunt. "It was really odd how we found the church. I'd like to talk to the real estate agent about that as well."

"Actually—" Aunt Martha blushed "—that was me. You see, the real estate agent is the daughter of a church friend of mine. When I found out she was showing you the Carringtons' old house, I asked her to give you the address to the church. I knew Blake was very curious about it before they moved, and though they had once gone to services there, it had been closed down for years. I fibbed a little to the Realtor and said you would understand, so I wouldn't have to explain to her what the address was for. I hoped you would, anyway."

"That was clever of you." Brynn giggled. "We thought she had set us up at first."

"But a little risky. How did you know she wouldn't say anything about it to the Parhams?" Avery couldn't seem to keep quiet any longer.

"I wasn't completely sure. But I suspected the church was important. I could only assume it had something to do with it. Blake announced very suddenly that he and Stephanie were going to move to Texas, and he'd been looking into some of the same things you were before they left. The church was the only thing I could think of that might hold answers."

"Did my adoptive and birth parents both attend church there?" Brynn was shaking her head at the odd circumstances of it all.

"Yes, but only briefly. Stephanie and Blake began attending church there shortly before the Carringtons moved. For a short time, though, they attended services together. So even if not for all the articles over the fire, Blake would begin to see Rebecca Carrington in you eventually. I did, too, and when I mentioned it, he knew others soon would, as well."

"What about the wall safe in the church? Would they have known about it somehow?" Avery asked this question.

Aunt Martha thought for a moment. "You know, I'd forgotten, but at one time, Rebecca

Carrington served as a volunteer office assistant in that church. And Anderson Carrington was on the church board. So yes, I suppose they would've probably had reason to know the combination."

A knock drew everyone's attention to the door. Avery opened it to reveal Wilder Hawthorne standing on the other side, welcomed him in and introduced everyone.

"I thought you'd want to know we found the leak providing the information to the DA as well." Wilder looked at Avery as he took the offered seat. "It seems Parham was paying a relative in the department to keep him apprised of everything that might affect him or his crimes. A Sergeant Joe Wilson, who also handled many of the cases you were suspicious of before. He worked with Luke Miller on the investigation of the Carringtons' fire as well."

"That's why there was such a cover-up and why Miller couldn't do a thorough investigation, then." Avery looked angry.

"And that's not all. When Rebecca Carrington began to report her suspicions that something was going on with the nursing homes, Wilson was responsible for looking into her findings. She must have somehow realized he was corrupt and started compiling evidence of her own to present to someone higher up." Wilder cleared his throat. "I tracked down some anonymous reports to the FBI about the local DA from around that time. Apparently they got to the Carringtons before they were able to provide the evidence to the FBI. They must have thought they destroyed the evidence in the fire."

"Then why come after Brynn? Why would she be a threat if they thought the evidence was gone?" Avery asked.

"When she arrived at Cargill House, the Parhams decided they had better cover their bases. It scared the wits out of them all to see Brynn in town, looking like Rebecca Carrington come back to life. The crimes of their past had truly come back to haunt them. I suppose they didn't want any reminders." Wilder shook his head sadly. "Then, when you guys started exploring the house on Cherry Blossom Street and the old church, they concluded there must still be some evidence out there."

"So my only real crime against them was reminding them too much of my mother?" Brynn laid a hand on her chest. "They were truly evil."

"They stole millions from insurance companies and the families of nursing home patients. It was quite an elaborate scam and they got very wealthy off it. Not to mention they could do anything they wanted with Clifford Parham serving as the district attorney."

"How will the authorities know if they got everyone who was involved?" Brynn asked. "He had to have had help to get away with all of his crimes, even if he was the DA."

"The FBI is going through everything in great detail. You can relax. They'll get everything," Wilder reassured her. "Now, if you'll excuse me, I need to get going."

When he opened the door to leave, they saw a brunette who waiting for him by a car outside.

"His FBI *friend*?" Brynn asked, waving toward the lovely woman, who stood smiling as she waited for Wilder.

Avery chuckled. "I guess so."

Brynn had disappeared into herself just before heading outside the boarding house to walk down the street. Avery watched her make her way slowly down the sidewalk, debating over whether or not he should follow her. She probably needed time to sort through her thoughts and make sense of everything that had happened. He couldn't imagine what she was feeling.

He tried to give her some space. He really did.

Finally, he couldn't stand it anymore. What if she slipped away? He couldn't stand the thought of her going back to Texas before he got a chance to tell her how he felt. He eased out of the now empty B and B and jogged down the sidewalk after her.

When he caught up to her, she paused, glancing at him with an expression of surprise. "What's wrong?"

"Brynn, I know you already have a lot on your mind. But I really need to talk to you." Avery didn't waste any time.

"I know this is unexpected. We are just getting to know each other again. But just the idea of letting you go is killing me. I can't let you go back to Texas without telling you how I feel. I meant it when I said I loved you. Stay. Teach here. Live close to your aunt. I'm not ready to let you go." Avery felt his stomach roll over, but he had to get the words out. He couldn't let her go.

Brynn's eyes welled up with tears. "I've been thinking the same things. I can't stand the idea of leaving you both so soon."

He stood and folded her into his arms. He kissed her with all the tenderness and longing he had been holding in for so many days. She returned his kiss with all the strength she had.

EPILOGUE

Tilley walked into the bridal dressing room to find Brynn thumbing through the old Carrington family Bible once more. She was reading Psalm 91 verse 15, one of the verses her mother had written in the prayer book and an old favorite of Brynn's. It made her feel more connected to Rebecca Carrington. Brynn offered her friend a rueful grin as she looked up, white fabric spilling around her legs where she sat in a pool of chiffon and lace.

"I can't help wishing they were here, even though I never really knew them. Somehow I feel like I did." Brynn fingered the pages with reverence, her neatly manicured fingers splayed across one side as if she could somehow absorb something of her parents.

"I have a feeling they're here with you in spirit. Both sets of parents." Tilley smiled, laying a hand across hers. "And right now, you have a whole crowd of Thorpes waiting at the end of the aisle for you. Heaven help anyone who tries to cause you any problems today. Or ever again, now that I think about it."

Avery had proposed a few short months after Brynn had moved back to Corduroy. She had learned she had inherited the house from the Carringtons and she had been working to restore and update it ever since.

On the first night of her arrival, which was shortly after the dust had settled, Tilley had been filled in on all the danger and excitement she had missed. She had quickly fallen in love with the area as well, and was convinced Brynn was doing the right thing by staying. That made it all that much easier for Brynn to convince her to stay and work with her. Brynn was going back to college because she planned to turn her birth parents' old house into a new adoption agency.

Once the papers in the safe deposit box were retrieved, they'd discovered that Brynn owned the house where they had found the box hidden in the stairs. It hadn't actually been the Parhams' to sell, but they had claimed it since it was still in her birth parents' names when they died. Neither of her parents had had remaining living relatives at the time aside from Brynn, so DA Parham had had no trouble convincing his underlings to make it legally his. But it had never been truly his.

Brynn felt it would be an appropriate legacy to her parents to open an adoption agency in the Carringtons' old house to help children find loving homes. She had enlisted the help of a friend who had worked in social services to help her get it started. She planned to call it the Carrington-Evans House, honoring both sets of her parents.

"I came to tell you it's time," Tilley announced. "Aunt Martha's waiting for you."

Brynn's aunt had agreed to walk her down the aisle in honor of her brother, who had raised Brynn. They followed Tilley and Brynn's two soon-to-be sisters-in-law down to meet Avery and his brothers, Briggs, Beau and Grayson. Her toddling niece-to-be Riley served as flower girl. Madison's middle curved out gracefully under her bridesmaid's dress and Lauren grinned at her happily.

The expression on Avery's face as she appeared in the aisle took her breath away. Her heart was overflowing. Everything had worked out better than she could ever have imagined. Though her parents weren't here, she felt the presence of all of them smiling down on her today, just as Tilley had said.

The only shadow over the whole event was

the fact that Caldwell, Avery's younger brother, hadn't responded to any of his texts, calls or emails. They had invited him to come and share their joy, despite the continued rift between the brothers. But Caldwell might as well be off the grid. No one had heard from him in weeks.

Now Avery kissed her sweetly in front of their guests as the ceremony ended, and as they made their way through the throng of guests to the outdoor reception on the family ranch, Grayson laid a hand on Avery's arm.

"I need to tell you something before the reception." He looked anxiously at Brynn. "Hopefully this will bring happiness and not pain on your special day."

Avery tilted his head slightly as he focused on Grayson. "What is it?"

"I just got a text from Caldwell. He says to wish you well." Grayson paused.

"I don't know why he didn't just tell me himself." Avery's face grew a little red, but he shook it off. No doubt he didn't want to let his brother anger him on this special day.

"I don't, either. But that isn't all." Grayson took a deep breath. "He's married, also. Just recently."

"And didn't have the grace to tell any of us? Grayson, what is going on with him?" Avery wasn't maintaining control as well as a few seconds before.

"I don't know. I didn't mean to cast a shadow over your day. I just thought you should know before you left for your honeymoon." Grayson shook his head. "I'm sorry for the poor timing."

"I appreciate that." He pulled Brynn closer. "Let's go greet everyone."

Soon, Caldwell's strange behavior was forgotten as they danced under the big Wyoming sky, surrounded by loved ones. The Thorpes had all embraced Brynn into their fold as if she had always been a part of it. She now had the family she had been missing of late, all of Avery's present brothers gathering protectively to adopt her as their new sister. And her new sisters-in-law had treated her as a friend they had known forever.

The guests began to dwindle at last, and as Avery led her away, Brynn realized just how very wonderful their life together was going to be.

Avery kissed her on the forehead. "I can't wait to spend the rest of my life with you, Brynn Thorpe. I love you."

"I feel exactly the same way. I am so grateful you are my husband. God has been so good to us." Brynn looked up into the sky. "I love you, too. I know my parents would have loved you as well. Both sets of them."

He chuckled. "I hope so. I certainly know they would be proud of you. You are an amazing woman."

"I had a lot of help from an amazing man." She smiled up into his dreamy blue eyes.

"I guess we make a pretty good pair." Avery kissed her, long and slow on the mouth this time.

When at last he released her, she breathed deeply of his love. Their foreheads connected as they stared into each other's eyes.

Brynn sighed. "For life."

* * * * *

If you liked this story from Sommer Smith, check out her previous Love Inspired Suspense books,

Under Suspicion
Attempted Abduction
Ranch Under Siege

Available now from Love Inspired Suspense! Find more great reads at www.LoveInspired.com

Dear Reader,

Avery and Brynn's story has been quite the journey for me. As soon the Thorpe brothers began to take shape, I knew Avery would be my favorite. He's always struggled with shyness in the shadow of his take-charge brothers, and he had to find out for himself that he was just as capable of being a hero. I have a soft spot for Brynn, also, because she is such a gentle soul but needs to understand who she really is, especially in the wake of her mother's deathbed confession. Add to that the crush she has always had on Avery Thorpe, and she's an equally endearing character to me.

Brynn finds determination within herself when she realizes that her birth parents have entrusted her with something important. Avery must decide if he will let his fear of failure win out or take a chance with Brynn. Sometimes the most difficult things God brings us through make the greatest impact on our lives. I hope you enjoyed their story.

There are two more Thorpe brothers with stories to come. Beau finds an enchanting new neighbor and her precocious little sister in danger and must come to their aid. And Caldwell is surrounded by secrets. Be on the lookout for these stories soon.

I always enjoy hearing from readers! My email address is ssmith.kgc3@gmail.com and you can find my author page on Facebook (Sommer N. Smith, Author) to stay up-to-date on news of upcoming books. Thank you for reading this story!

Blessings,
Sommer Smith

Get 4 FREE REWARDS!

We'll send you 2 FREE Books plus 2 FREE Mystery Gifts.

FREE Value Over **$20**

Both the **Love Inspired®** and **Love Inspired® Suspense** series feature compelling novels filled with inspirational romance, faith, forgiveness and hope.

YES! Please send me 2 FREE novels from the Love Inspired or Love Inspired Suspense series and my 2 FREE gifts (gifts are worth about $10 retail). After receiving them, if I don't wish to receive any more books, I can return the shipping statement marked "cancel." If I don't cancel, I will receive 6 brand-new Love Inspired Larger-Print books or Love Inspired Suspense Larger-Print books every month and be billed just $6.49 each in the U.S. or $6.74 each in Canada. That is a savings of at least 16% off the cover price. It's quite a bargain! Shipping and handling is just 50¢ per book in the U.S. and $1.25 per book in Canada.* I understand that accepting the 2 free books and gifts places me under no obligation to buy anything. I can always return a shipment and cancel at any time by calling the number below. The free books and gifts are mine to keep no matter what I decide.

Choose one: ☐ **Love Inspired**
Larger-Print
(122/322 IDN GRHK)

☐ **Love Inspired Suspense**
Larger-Print
(107/307 IDN GRHK)

Name (please print)

Address   Apt. #

City   State/Province   Zip/Postal Code

Email: Please check this box ☐ if you would like to receive newsletters and promotional emails from Harlequin Enterprises ULC and its affiliates. You can unsubscribe anytime.

Mail to the **Harlequin Reader Service:**
IN U.S.A.: P.O. Box 1341, Buffalo, NY 14240-8531
IN CANADA: P.O. Box 603, Fort Erie, Ontario L2A 5X3

Want to try 2 free books from another series! Call 1-800-873-8635 or visit www.ReaderService.com.

*Terms and prices subject to change without notice. Prices do not include sales taxes, which will be charged (if applicable) based on your state or country of residence. Canadian residents will be charged applicable taxes. Offer not valid in Quebec. This offer is limited to one order per household. Books received may not be as shown. Not valid for current subscribers to the Love Inspired or Love Inspired Suspense series. All orders subject to approval. Credit or debit balances in a customer's account(s) may be offset by any other outstanding balance owed by or to the customer. Please allow 4 to 6 weeks for delivery. Offer available while quantities last.

Your Privacy—Your information is being collected by Harlequin Enterprises ULC, operating as Harlequin Reader Service. For a complete summary of the information we collect, how we use this information and to whom it is disclosed, please visit our privacy notice located at corporate.harlequin.com/privacy-notice. From time to time we may also exchange your personal information with reputable third parties. If you wish to opt out of this sharing of your personal information, please visit readerservice.com/consumerschoice or call 1-800-873-8635. **Notice to California Residents**—Under California law, you have specific rights to control and access your data. For more information on these rights and how to exercise them, visit corporate.harlequin.com/california-privacy.

LIRLIS22R3

COUNTRY LEGACY COLLECTION

19 FREE BOOKS IN ALL!

Cowboys, adventure and romance await you in this new collection! Enjoy superb reading all year long with books by bestselling authors like Diana Palmer, Sasha Summers and Marie Ferrarella!